I0576371

HALO ROBERTS

Finding My Safe

A Second Chance Romantic Comedy

Second edition

ISBN: 978-1-7770505-9-7

Cover art by Teshia Saunders
Advisor: Terri Stepek

This book was professionally typeset on Reedsy.
Find out more at reedsy.com

This one is for me. Cheers to those all night writing binges, because the story wants to find life on the page. They give me faith that the words will always be there when I need them.

Love is in the water,
love is in the air,
show me where to look,
tell me will love be there?

-Shine, Collective Soul

Contents

Meet You at the Hen Party

***

W^{ren}

Bachelorette parties suck. Elbowing my way through the crowded bar, I curse Gran for teaching me manners as a child. If it weren't for her, I would have given this whole night a hard pass. Instead, here I am, getting another round of shots for Jenna and her friends who can, at best, be called acquaintances from med school. Squeezing between a rock and a hard place; in the form of a man so firmly wedged onto his stool that I question if he died a few days ago and a trucker with a sun-dried tomato for a face who sighs and moves ever so slightly, I wave at the bartender and glance around.

You know that no-man's land where the country meets the city? You're driving through street lights and neighborhoods and BAM, nothing for about a mile before the fields and barns start? That's where Joe's Bar sits, right smack in the middle of that city-country deadzone. It's a pretty average crappy bar, full of hard-drinking regulars, the occasional hipsters who roll in looking for an experience, bar flies who reek of cheap perfume and desperation, and a party of silly girls hogging up the tiny dance floor. *That's me. I'm with the silly girls.*

Waving at the bartender again, I walk myself back through the conversation that brought me to this point. Jenna approached me earlier today with the friendliest smile I'd ever seen on her face. *There's the mistake...I fell for that crocodile smile.* She fed me some kind of sob story about Monica not having many local friends who would throw her a hen party, *boo-freakin-hoo, I fell for that too.* Yep, and now here I am, buying a round for these silly drunks I barely know. *I should bail.*

"Hurry up Wren!! We're sooooo thirsty!" Monica trills, dancing in a circle with her stupid plastic champagne glass held high. She's gaining the attention of the pool players nearby. Pausing their game to look at her, the nearest one grins at his friends and loops an arm around her waist as she dances by, pulling her in tight. *Oh great, this could get bad fast.* I'm too far away to hear what he's saying, but her smile quickly fades and she starts squirming free, so it's not hard to guess at his intentions.

Jenna stomps over, finger raised in a very official angry point to give him a piece of her mind, but one of his buddies twirls her into his arms, laughing rudely as she squeals indignantly. I glance at the bartender who gives a decidedly overworked sigh. Picking up his phone from under the bar, he appears to check the time before tossing the phone on the counter and continuing to pour drinks.

"Thanks bud, you're a big help," I grumble as I shove away from the bar and make my way back through the crowd. I can see angry tears brimming in Monica's eyes as she swats away the offending hands of the dipshit who won't leave her alone. *See now, that's not fair...and this is her hen party damnit...* Pasting a smile on my face I put a little bounce in my step, *all the better to get close to you losers.* The two men who are bothering the girls see me coming and glance at each other before smiling at me.

"Well good evening Sugar," the one bothering Monica lets go of her waist, tipping an invisible hat at me, his voice oily as his eyes scan me top to tail. It doesn't take him long, I'm five foot nothing, and I walk right up close while he gets an eye-full. Not wasting a beat, I get in his space, grab his nuts, and squeeze. Hard. As his smile quickly turns to an open-mouthed bellow of pain, he curls in on himself trying to get away from me. I help the momentum along, pushing his head straight down on the edge of the pool table with a satisfying thunk and he falls to the floor, dazed, holding his squished nuts. *Just like you taught me Gran.*

"What the hell?!" His buddy lets Jenna loose and looks back and forth from his fallen friend to me several times in rapid succession. *Now to get us out of this mess.*

"You stupid jackasses," I fill my normally sweet Southern voice with as much disdain as I can drum up. "Do you know who these girls' Daddies are?" I point at Jenna, Monica and Courtney, "CEO, Senator, Sheriff, and you think you can just paw their *baby girls*?" Idiot number one is still on the floor, but his buddies are backing away looking seriously uncomfortable.

I shake my head in disgust. "Apologize and get back to your game, you hear?" They mumble 'sorry' and turn back to the pool table shame-faced, but the idiot on the floor isn't quite ready to give up.

"Whatever bitch," he groans, climbing painfully to his feet,

3

eyes narrowed. *Damnit.*

Turning to the girls, I decide to herd them to the door and find a bouncer to walk us to our car. A hard poke in the shoulder turns me back to the angry idiot with sore nuts.

"We ain't done yet sweetie," he leers, confidence returning, as he reaches out a finger to twirl a strand of my blonde hair. I swat him away, angry. As I'm deciding whether to dust off a few more tricks Gran taught me or just insist that the bartender get off his ass and call the cops or something, Sore Nuts jerks his hand away like he touched a hot stove.

"My apologies, we thought you girls wanted to dance. We're just going to play pool now and leave you be." His words tumble out in a rush, fear in his eyes as he stares over my head. *The hell?*

"Hey Kane, didn't know you were working tonight," Sore Nuts continues, trying to sound calm. *Kane? Ohmygod.* I whirl around and almost bash my nose into a very hard chest covered in a flannel work shirt. Taking a tiny step back I look up and see a grim face I'd recognize anywhere. He doesn't glance at me as he gives Sore Nuts a hard look.

"Roy, Charlie," he rumbles, looking at each of them in turn. "Looks like your game is over." He sets his jaw, I can see the muscles working under his beard. It's shorter than I remember it, he used to keep it long, now it's just barely long enough to grab. *That's not a weird measurement at all, where did that come from, wow.* Darker red, almost brown, as if he's not in the sun as much as he used to be when he worked on the farm. *His hair used to be such a golden red, I always thought he looked like a lion. I wonder if he remembers me.*

"Yeahhhh, I got an early shift tomorrow," Roy's voice startles me and I turn and watch as he stretches his arms overhead and

4

gives a fake yawn, "better call it." Trying to save face, Charlie nods and they head for the door. The men they were with don't even glance my way as they return to their pool game. I turn back to Kane and he looks down at me, recognition sparking in his eyes.

It's been almost four years since I last saw him, but I'd know those eyes anywhere. Hazel with green and blue flecks, he's got light lashes, thick and long. Almost pretty if the rest of him weren't so *man*. I don't know how tall he is, but I'm staring him in the sternum, so he's way over 6'. Thick muscles roll under the work shirt, wide neck, broad shoulders, he's built like a bull but he moves like a fighter. My grandad would've had eyes on him in a minute, ready to get him in the ring.

"Hi Kane, it's been a while." I realize we haven't said anything yet and the words whisper out. The tiniest smile edges up the corner of his mouth.

"Wren." He's always quiet, no extra words needed, so I'm actually a little surprised when he continues, "You're a long way from Gravity."

"So are you," I counter, "no one knew where you went, you just up and left…" trailing off, I don't know what else to say. I'd known him because Gravity was a small town. I'd been dating a guy he worked with and met him just once. The next day, Kane was gone. *Leaving me memories of a dance, the feel of his lips pressing into my hair, and a slightly-confused broken heart.*

"Yeah, um…Mike with you?" He shifts his shoulders uncomfortably and glances around as I blurt out a little laugh.

"That's a no, he figured out I was actually going to go to college and knocked up Ella Harkins before my end of the truck seat was cold." It doesn't even hurt, I haven't thought about Mike in a long time.

5

"Sorry," Kane frowns, like I'm going to cry or something, and I laugh again.

"Nothing to be sorry for, Mike is a memory at this point, he was fun to date right after high school while I was taking classes and saving." I toss my hair back over my shoulder and decide to try again. "So why did you leave Gravity without sayin' a word?"

"So med school?" His voice cuts across mine, throwing me off. At the same time Jenna's voice drowns us both out.

"Oh my god Wren you were so cave-girl with that guy! That was in-*sane*! I'm totally pissed I didn't get a clip of that to post!" Her lip pouts out and while she takes a breath she gives Kane an eye-banging and bumps her shoulder into mine. "Aren't you going to introduce me?" *No, I don't want to and get your eyes back in your fool head, Jenna.*

"Jenna, Kane. Kane, Jenna." I try to keep my voice friendly and barely succeed. A happy little butterfly herd fills my chest when his eyes barely flick her way. He gives her a nod and ignores her outstretched hand. Leaning down, his mouth close enough to my ear that I feel his breath tickling my skin, I can hear the smile he's hiding.

"It was good to see you Wren, I'm sorry I didn't say goodbye." He doesn't glance at either of us again as he turns and shoulders his way through the crowd, leaving us staring at his back.

"What a dick." Jenna sniffs, turning away. I nod bemusedly and follow her back to the dance floor.

A Dance and a Song

K ane

Gravity, Georgia had been a good place to get away. My old man was always in trouble with the wrong people and I was tired of the guilt he piled on while he somehow found ways to blame me for his debt. I sure as fuck wasn't going to follow his path and be a washed up fighter, old before my time.

I'd gone to stay with an aunt, she was my mother's sister, and there was no love lost between her and my old man. I told her I didn't want him to know I was there and she just nodded, business as usual. She was newly widowed, needed help with odd jobs and paying rent.

I hired on at a huge farming operation, the boss was a good man, fair, easy to respect. It was good work for me. I've always been strong, I like working hard, working until I'm not thinking, just letting the muscles take over until the job's done.

My aunt eventually moved on with a boyfriend, but I stayed, took over the payments on her little house full of odds and ends she didn't want anymore. Got to know the guys at the farm, they were always up for a beer on the tailgate at the end of a long day. I'd been there a few months when one night a guy I was working with, Mike, told me to come with him and this girl he was bringing to a street dance in town.

For some reason I said I would go, and found myself in his truck headed to the dance. He pulled off on a side street before we got there, and walked up to a tiny yellow house, cheerful, lots of flowers. Before he could knock, this little blonde popped out the door and he slung an arm around her shoulders for the walk to the truck. Thick, straight hair fluttered down her back almost to her waist. Her eyes were blue, almost too big for her face with its little pointy chin.

She'd startled the tiniest bit when I got out and then smiled and hopped in, scooting to the middle between Mike and I. She was wearing jean shorts and a little checkered shirt with buttons. Her thigh was warm right through my jeans when her leg rested up against mine.

In books and movies and stuff, people talk about hearing music or birds singing or a choir of angels or some shit when they fall in love. *Well that's garbage and none of that happened.* I felt like a lead balloon had dropped into the pit of my stomach so hard it sent a jolt to my junk. As the smell of her perfume and whatever flowers were in her shampoo washed over me, I felt heat climbing up my neck. I was sitting in that truck, with the most perfect girl I'd ever seen...and her date.

She'd leaned back and turned so she could look up at me, and shyly held out her hand. I was afraid there would be a sonic boom when I touched her, but apparently I'm the only one who felt it because we just shook hands.

"I'm Wren," her soft voice tied up the perfect girl package with a big damn bow. I grunted, "Kane," like a fucking gorilla.

"Nice to meet ya," she smiled and then turned to fiddle with the radio.

Later that night, Wren wandered back by the bar where I was avoiding a pair of women who kept hauling me out to dance and grab my ass. She parked her cute little butt on the stool next to me with a sigh. I'd waved at the bartender to bring her a beer and she'd smiled and taken a sip before sighing again.

"Where's Mike?" The words slipped out before I could stop myself. *I didn't give a shit about Mike.* But Mike was one of the few friends I had, and they were together.

"Oh he's talking to the guys, I think he's had enough dancing," her lip pouted out just a tiny bit and she'd glanced at me out of the corner of her eye.

"Have you?" *What am I doing?*

"Oh, well…it's a lot more fun with a partner." She turned and looked me in the eyes, and before I could think, I held out my hand. Her cheeks pinked up, but she put her hand in mine and we walked out to the dance floor. The music was loud and a fast song was playing, I didn't let go of her hand as I whirled her around, smiling at her little squeal of delight.

The women who came and went in a steady stream through my old man's house were of all shapes, sizes and temperaments, but he always seemed to pick the ones that loved to dance. I'd spent many nights in the kitchen listening to his current woman curse him while she tossed back a bottle of wine. It usually ended in a dance lesson, *and a lot of advice on how not to treat a woman.*

Wren spun in my arms like we'd been dancing together

9

forever. Her blonde hair fanned out behind her as she laughed, trusting me to lead. We danced for two songs, and then the music slowed and the singer started belting out an old love song. I wasn't sure if she wanted to keep dancing until she stepped forward and put a hand on my shoulder, her other hand hovering in mid-air until I took it and slid my other arm around her waist. She was so short that her arm was stretched up funny to reach my shoulder and I heard her laugh under her breath. Her hand started a slow slide down my arm until finally she slid her arm around my waist.

My world stopped.

I felt her fingers start to play along the muscles of my back. I held her like she was made of glass, but I wanted to pull her in tight. Feeling a tiny hum against my chest, I realized she was singing along. Leaning my head down to listen, her voice strengthened as she lost herself in the song.

Love is in the water
  Love is in the air
  Show me where to look
  Tell me will love be there

She lost the words for a minute, but kept humming along. I was bent down close enough to kiss her hair, and that seemed like a hell of a good idea, so I lost my mind and pressed my lips in her hair that smelled like honey and sunshine. Just a tiny kiss, and then I felt a tap on the back of my shoulder.

"Thanks man, I needed a beer break," Mike laughed. My arms dropped away from Wren and I took a step back with a nod. She looked almost dazed and smiled at me before turning to Mike.

"Maybe you should take some lessons," she told him cheekily, tossing me a wink before letting him pull her in close. I walked back to the bar before I did something stupid. *My heart badly wanted me to punch Mike's smiling face in, and tell him to get his hands off my girl, but given the circumstances that seemed unreasonable.*

Ten hours later I got a phone call. I told my boss I had to leave town, family emergency. I packed my truck and drove away from Gravity without looking back. *I looked up the song later...Shine, Collective Soul, played it until I knew every word by heart. It was like taking a tiny piece of Wren with me.*

Blindsided

❦

*K*ane

The hardest thing I'd ever done was driving out of Gravity four years ago without finding her one more time. Until tonight, when I walked away from her again. It doesn't make any sense, I barely knew her, but those blue eyes stared straight into my soul and I was ready to rip my heart out and hand it to her for safekeeping. *Why? Because I'm a fucking idiot, falling in love with a girl over a dance and a song.*

Heading to the back of the bar, I give the bartender, John, a nod to keep an eye on things and head for the office, shoving the door shut behind me. Leaning on the desk, I try to make some sense of what just happened. Some twist of fate brought Wren back across my path. She remembered me, even seemed upset that I'd left…and I walked away again. *What the hell is wrong with me, I'm given a second chance and I run away and hide?*

Not this time.

Standing, I hope she and her friends are still out dancing. Striding to the door I head back up the hall, laughing to myself as I think about her. The confidence in her step as she walked right up to that idiot Roy and squeezed his junk until I thought his eyes were going to pop right out of his head. Followed it with a header to the pool table, smooth as it goes. There's more to her than blonde hair and big blue eyes.

As I start to wade through the crowd, John flags me down, a worried look on his face. With a quick glance at the dance floor, I see Wren is still here. She's leaning on the side rail with her arms crossed, laughing as the women she's with flail around in a drunken dance. Changing course, I head over to the bar, leaning over it just enough to hear John over the music.

"You better keep an eye on those boys over there," John's nervous, his eyes darting around as he points out a group of two men and two women near the pinball machine. I recognize them, rough crew, but they don't usually cause any trouble. Then one of the women stands up and starts to do a lap-dance for one of the men.

"Yeah, see…that's not her man," John nods at the other hall leading to the bathrooms where another man is just walking out, scratching at his beard and bumping into the wall. He's walking like he's on a boat in rough water, and obviously had a few too many. *Well shit.*

"What the fuck are you doing Brenda?" He bellows across the room when he spots them, pushing his way through the crowd. Brenda flips him off and continues her dance. The man she's wiggling around on laughs and shoves her away just enough to stand up, pulling her close again with a possessive hand on her ass.

"Looks like she's doing me tonight," he scoffs and the

13

boyfriend doesn't utter another word, he just dives at the other man and the fight is on. I'm wading through the crowd, still too far away to break it up before it really gets started. One of the women grabs a pool cue and starts swinging away, shrieking like a banshee, and everyone backs up.

"Put the stick down." I growl at the woman. She drops it. I point at a chair out of harm's way. "Go sit down." She goes, dragging her man away from his spot at the edge of the fight. The second woman isn't ready to give up so easy, she's in the tangle of men, pulling the hair of one, screeching about how she's a lady and he's going to treat her like one. I'm not even sure she knows who's hair she's got a hold of, but they're going to have a bald spot when she's done.

Troy, the other bouncer who's been on the door, arrives at the same time. He carefully comes in behind the woman, bear hugs her to avoid her long-ass fingernails, and lifts her off the men, leaving me with a tangle of bloody drunks to sort.

Unfortunately for the idiots rolling around on the floor, I glance at the door just in time to see Wren's blonde hair as she leaves. I'm glad she isn't in harm's way, these fights can spread quickly, but now I'm pissed. Grabbing each of the men by the back of the shirt, I pull them away from each other and lift them up. I hear a 'whoa' uttered by the buddy who was smart enough not to jump in the brawl, and I realize one of the guys I'm holding is completely off the floor. I give them each a hard shake.

"You done rollin' around like a couple of dumbasses?" They don't answer, one just hangs there, the other takes a half-hearted swing at me. I shake him again and jerk my head at the door. Troy nods and herds the other three idiots behind me. I carry/drag the two fighters to the door and shove them into the parking lot. Standing in between them, I stare at the one who's still got some fight left in him while Troy looks the other members of the group over, deciding to talk to the man who wasn't fighting.

"You sober? If not, call a ride. You're not coming back in, and if either of those two idiots tries to drive, I'm calling the cop that lives down the road." The man sullenly pulls out his phone. A woman answers and when she gets done chewing his ass off, he disconnects.

"His woman'll be here in a few minutes." He mutters, jerking his head at one of the bleeders. *Already got a woman at home? He's in for a bad night.*

"Alright. I'm good here Kane," Troy takes up a spot near the door where he can watch them until they clear out. I head back in the bar.

* * *

I'm no stranger to fighting. I grew up on the edge of the ring, watching my old man fight, watching the arenas turn into small town rings, and finally shitty bars and underground clubs. He was washed out long before he gave up, never really made it big, never knew when to quit.

My mom was the glue that held us together, but she died when I was ten, car accident. By then he was getting throwaway matches that made him about fifty bucks. He was lucky if he came home with anything after he paid the bartender. I was still going to his fights, mostly to help him get home after, and he was a mean drunk.

One night when I was 17, he took a swing at me, a real punch not just trying to shove me or toss a hit at my shoulder, he went for my face. It was like time stopped for a split second. I leaned back, easily dodging it, and then gave him a hard tap in the ribs. The air rushed out of him along with all the fight and he stared at me for a solid minute while he got his breath back.

"Why the hell ain't we been training you for these, boy?" I remember how the words wheezed out of him painfully, and I was disgusted. I turned and walked away, but getting me in the ring became his new obsession.

In some ways it was good. He cleaned up and got a job, *he wanted to be able to get me in a gym, and those aren't free.* I was getting bigger every day, I'd always been big and tall, but I started really bulking up, and I was fast. It was fun to train and workout at the gym. I took to fighting like a duck to water, I guess it was in my blood, my old man said so often enough.

Soon enough, I turned 18 and I was entered in some matches, little, local stuff. I won. Everytime. So the spotlight centered on me. I was getting a lot of attention and everything was going well. I noticed some guys hanging at the ring talking to my old man a lot. I didn't like the looks of them, but he always said they were just talking 'business' and not to worry about it.

One night I was in a match at a small casino, and those same guys were there. We were pretty far from home, and my dad was acting shifty. He kept acting like everything was fine, but they came back to the training room where I was getting taped up. They told me to play with the guy I was going to fight, drag it out to the third round. There was money in it for me if I kept the fight going until the third round. After they left the room, Dad stared at the floor for a while.

"You should just do it, Kane." He finally looked up at me and then right back down at the floor, uncomfortable. "They didn't ask you to throw the match…just make it take a little longer."

"What happens if I don't?" He didn't like my question, his shoulders hunched up and he barked a laugh.

"Well I'm sure that'd be a problem, son." He looked at me again, fear creeping into his eyes. "Yes, I expect that'd be a problem." He sighed.

I made the fight last until the third round. I didn't talk to him for days after, so angry that he was weak and always writing checks his ass couldn't cash. That wasn't the first time I had to 'decide' the outcome of a fight. I was big, strong, young, and fast. I was going to win, it was almost too easy.

His 'friends' started showing up more often. Started throwing parties after the matches, sending girls to my hotel room, trying to get me hooked on something. I sent the women away, disgusted. Avoided the booze and the drugs. Not my old man, he partied hard and damn near killed himself. I had to scrape him off the floor most mornings. I told him more than once that I was done, but I was a damn kid, no plan, no help, and *he made sure,* no money.

The day I'd been dreading finally came. Jerick Smythe, *Smitty, the boss himself,* showed up at the gym. Told me it was time to pay my dues. They had a new fighter that they wanted to bill as my rival. Start the whole thing off with me losing a match.

"The fall of the giant will be heard for miles," he said. "We'll sell so many tickets to the grudge match your head will spin," he said. Smitty threw on all the guilt trips and lightly-veiled threats he could think of, and I started planning.

I told my old man he shouldn't come, they could probably tie that into some damn gossip about why I lost.

"Yeah, I don't want to watch you get your ass kicked anyway, they must see something better in this new kid than they do in you," was his sneering response as he stared into his beer.

The night of the fight, my old man was dead-ass drunk on the floor of the kitchen, girlfriend-of-the-month fussing over him, when I walked out of his house.

I didn't lose the fight.

The crowd was waiting for me to get my gloves off and come back into the ring for pictures and the interview, no idea that anything was wrong. That was the only window I had, and I took it. I'd barely gotten my gloves off, ignoring the furious looks from Smitty and his women sitting in the front row. I walked straight to a table in the corner and got my winnings from the bookie I'd talked to just before the fight. I didn't even go back to the training room, I walked out of the casino in my shorts, jumped in my truck and roared off down the road.

I managed to stay away for a while.

The day after I met Wren, I got a call from a number I didn't recognize. She says her name is Shelly and she called all the numbers in my Dad's phone trying to find me. She convinced my aunt it was an emergency and got my number. Then she put Smitty on the line.

"Your old man doesn't know when to quit," Smitty's voice snarls down the line. "Owes me a shit-ton of money, keeps promising you're going to come back, work off all the money you lost me with that stunt of yours." He kept talking, and I felt myself losing the life I had just started building in Gravity like a physical blow to the gut.

I went back to Louisiana, saw my old man in the hospital, and headed back to the gym. Nothing but a guard dog on a leash now. One afternoon, Smitty came to the gym, told me to go for a ride with him. We pulled up outside a dumpy little house and he glanced at me before looking at the house.

"The shit-pile living in that house owes me $500, Kane. Get it for me and I'll take it off your tab." He didn't look at me again, just pulled out a cigarette and lit it, cracking his window open.

I stared at him for a second. He was serious. My 'tab' was the gambling debt my old man had run up in the back room of a bar Smitty owned. I could have just walked away, it wasn't my problem. But when I walked into that hospital and saw my old man in that bed after a beating, I couldn't just walk away. I'd thought of my mom and how much she'd loved him, and I decided to do this one thing. I'd get him clear and then I was in the wind. One time, that's all.

I walked up to that house and in the door without knocking. Looking back, I'm lucky I didn't get my ass shot. The man inside was so scared when he saw me that he pissed himself, and his woman ran to the bathroom and came back out with a jar of money from the toilet tank. She was beating his head and shoulders with a pancake flipper when I walked back out of the house.

I pulled the money out of the jar as I walked up the sidewalk and tossed the jar in the yard. Getting back in the truck, I handed Smitty the money without a word.

"See, you're a natural, Kane." Smitty smiled around the cigarette in his lips and pulled away from the curb. We visited five more houses that day. I didn't have to hurt anyone. When you're as big as I am, a hard look makes people pretty sure you *will* hurt them, and that's usually enough.

Six months later, I'd paid off my old man's debt. I walked into Smitty's office and handed him the last grand. He'd tucked it away with a smile, and then steepled his fingers in front of him on his old green metal desk like we were in the Oval Office or something.

"I think we need to talk about you getting back in the ring, Kane." The tone of his voice put me on guard.

"I'm not fighting." *It'll never end, he thinks he's got me.*

"Well that wouldn't be good for your dad's health Kane, not good at all." He looked like a shark when he smiled.

"You're going to have to take that up with him, I guess. I'm done." I'd bluffed, and I'd walked out the door, calling my old man before I got to my truck. He left town, went to stay with an old girlfriend in Vegas. I got in the truck I'd already packed that morning and drove west until I was hungry. I'd stopped at this lonely bar along the side of the road somewhere in east Texas for a beer and a burger and got talking to the owner, Joe. He'd hired me on the spot.

* * *

And that could have been it. The money was paid and we were nobody. Smitty would have let it go. But, because my old man's a dip-shit of the highest order, he decided to swing by Smitty's house before he left town, knowing I'd just left Smitty at the bar.

He walked into the man's house and stole a wad of cash and a ring off the counter. A final 'piss off'. Unfortunately, the ring had a family crest on it and had been in Smitty's family for generations. The *really* unfortunate part is that my old man was blind drunk when he pulled this stunt, and he also used a handy bottle of ketchup to write, "Fuck Off" on the counter.

I got a call when I was about an hour down the road. I didn't answer. Predictably, Smitty was furious and wanted his hands on both of us.

"You bring that piece of dog-shit father of yours and my ring back. Now." He wasn't yelling, his voice was so quiet. I called my old man, but he was in the middle of a bender and couldn't speak complete words, much less sentences. When I finally talked to him a couple of days later, he was relatively sober and had no recollection of the ring, his best guess was that he'd pawned it.

* * *

That's why I walked away from Wren again. It's probably for the best that she left before I could talk to her, ask her to dance, *try to make her mine.* I work, I eat, I sleep. That's it. I'm keeping my head down and making some bank. I've got nothing to offer a woman but problems.

The rest of the night passes without any more excitement. When last call is finally over, Troy and I clear the bar. He watches the waitresses get to their cars and heads out through the front. I walk back through the bar, turning off lights and locking the office. My mind is full of long blonde hair, big blue eyes and a song as I grab my black leather jacket off a hook in the back hall. I shrug it on and walk outside, breathing in deep that cool night air.

Pain explodes through my left eye as I feel a bottle shatter on the ridge of my eyebrow. Swinging blind, I connect hard with a bearded jaw and hear a strangled yell as the man stumbles back. My vision is red, I can't see anything and something is very wrong with my left eye.

"Fucking make me...look...fucking stupid in front of that bitch.." I hear more slurred cursing from the man I hit, and then the crunch of gravel as he moves away from me. There's a roar as he starts up a truck, and I flatten my back against the building, not sure if he's leaving or planning to run my ass over for good measure.

He spins out of the alley fast, tossing some gravel close enough that I feel it hit my boots. Listening hard, I'm sure he's gone and I'm alone. Bleeding. Blind.

An Unexpected Patient

**

W^{ren}

The hen party went off without any further glitches. A little later in the evening, a couple of drunks got in a fight, so we left. I didn't see Kane again. I don't know why I care, but I can't get over seeing him again after such a long time. *That's not true. I care because I never forgot him, and there's no Mike to cut in this time.* I might go out to that old bar again this weekend, see if he's there.

Jenna's chattering away in my ear. I guess the party cemented our friendship, and we're just about to meet up with the doctor we're going on rounds with this dreary Monday morning. As soon as Dr. Silva arrives, it's game on. She's a stern woman with iron gray hair cut in a neat bob. Jenna immediately stops chatting as Dr. Silva puts on her glasses, gives us each a nod of approval for being punctual, and we move quickly through the halls.

The doctor fires questions at us, occasionally giving a nod of approval or a small sigh of annoyance. As we enter the first patient's room, Jenna gives me a quick smile of encouragement, we're going to make it, we're getting more nods than sighs today. The morning starts to fly by, I glance at the clock, it's almost 10 am and we've only got six rooms to go. Brushing at a stray hair that keeps escaping my pony tail, I follow Jenna into the next room.

It's Kane. My eyes don't want to register what I'm seeing for a minute and I stare at him in shock before it registers that the doctor has started talking about his condition. His eyes are closed and the left one is bandaged. It looks as if they've put tape along the lash line of the right eye to keep him from blinking it open. Small cuts on his forehead and eyelid that have been stitched and glued. I start paying attention at that point, listening to every word the doctor says.

"Tell me what you see Donovan." Dr. Silva's cool voice is quiet, Kane appears to be sleeping. Handing the chart to Jenna, the doctor looks at me. I walk closer to the edge of the bed and take in the damage.

"Lacerations to his eyebrow, eyelid, side of his cheek and shoulder have been repaired. It looks like all but two of the lacerations are superficial and will heal with minimal scarring." Behind the doctor, Jenna nods with a small smile as I continue. "The trauma must have extended to his eyes as one is bandaged and the other taped along the lash line to keep him from blinking it open." *Ohmygod what happened to his beautiful eyes.*

"The bruising suggests a potential concussion, and the soft cast on his right upper extremity suggests a potential fracture." My voice shakes the tiniest bit and the doctor glances at me.

"Accurate assessment Donovan. As for the right arm, you're

correct, we need to rule out a Brawler's Fracture when the swelling goes down. Nichols? Tell me if you've heard of a Brawler's Fracture?" I tune out again as Jenna starts to discuss fractures of the fourth and fifth metacarpals, and the fiberglass cast that might need to be put on tomorrow when the swelling is reduced. The doctor's next words grab my attention and a chill races up the backs of my arms.

"The most serious issue facing our young man is that the lacerations to his face were caused by a glass bottle. His left eye received trauma, and his right eye had multiple small shards of glass in it when he arrived. We've repaired what we can, we're keeping the muscles relaxed and the eyes closed. Only time will tell if his vision has been irreparably damaged." Walking to the door, the doctor opens it and continues down the hall.

Glancing back at Kane before I leave the room, I see his jaw tighten and his left hand curls into a helpless fist on the bed beside him. I don't know if he could hear me, or the doctor's words, but my heart breaks as I close the door softly.

The rest of the morning passes in a blur, we make it through rounds and then quick-walk back for a clinical meeting. By the end of the afternoon I'm starving, and can't stop thinking about Kane.

"Late lunch?" Jenna's voice cuts into my musings as we change out of scrubs, "I think they've got chicken pot pies today, they're palatable." *Palatable,* I laugh to myself as I picture my Gran's face if she were ever to meet Jenna. Jenna's really pretty nice, she's just a full-on princess who happens to have the brains to match her daddy's money.

"Sure, I'm starving," we walk to the cafeteria together, making small talk about the schedule for the week. I've got so many hours I may as well just sleep at the hospital, but that's part of the deal.

When I was a kid, I thought I wanted to be a nurse. In my Gran's world, women were nurses and men were doctors. It was an honorable profession, she said. I agreed. I always did like to care for people, and blood and stuff like that never did bother me.

Ma and Gran were over the moon when I got a job as a personal assistant for a woman who had come to Gravity to start a line of organic accessories for a major cosmetics company. Veronica Rockford blew into town like a tornado, bought a building, married a big farmer and put Gravity right on the map.

When she first came to town, she hired me to run errands and do office jobs for her, which was amazing because I was able to leave a completely shit job at a dive bar. I learned so much about business and being a stronger person and started really thinking about my future. I had taken a lot of my general education classes at a community college and online, *as much as I could afford*. I was reaching the point where I needed to decide if I was going to follow through and finish college, or stay in Gravity and see where this job with Veronica would lead.

One day Veronica called me into her office and made the decision for me. I remember thinking she looked awfully serious, and I wondered what was wrong.

"Wren, it's time we talk about your future," she said, dark eyes always assessing as they wandered my face. I remember feeling a nervous little quiver deep in my stomach as she continued.

"As much as I hate to lose you, I know you were planning for college when I hired you. Have you thought about what you would like to do?" Her fingers steepled before her, she waited for me to answer.

"Well," clearing my throat nervously, I tried to order my thoughts, "I always wanted to help people, I'd really like to be a doctor, but nursing school is probably better, I can't afford-," she cut me off.

"Let's assume you can, Wren, a doctor you say? I think that's an excellent choice for you, start your applications. I'm going to take care of the rest." She nodded to finalize the matter and then looked at my face. I was sitting there staring at her open-mouthed.

"I'm sorry, I should have eased you into that…let's try again." She started smiling and talked a little slower. "Wren, I'm going to send you to college, I'm giving you a scholarship. You've more than earned it working for me." Veronica had smiled gently at me. "I'm afraid my subtle button is broken. You're a wonderful girl and I am beyond tempted to try to keep you here, but you need to go and be a success in your own right."

"Okay," I whispered, still trying to get a handle on the moment.

"When you finish we'll open a new clinic, or even a hospital, here if you want to come home. I'm going to miss you." Veronica continued and then she trailed off and laughed at my expression.

I finally shut my mouth so hard my teeth clicked together. I couldn't find any words, so I lost my mind and dove at her, squeezing her in a hug as tears streamed down my cheeks. The normally cool and aloof, *and very UN-touchy-feely,* Veronica hugged me back, and I'm pretty sure we both wiped away a few tears.

So, my Cinderella story is that I volunteered for years of study and insane hours at the hospital, expenses paid by a woman who has enough money that she tossed out the idea of building a *hospital* the way some people might suggest building a mailbox.

Sometimes I still can't believe it, but it's seeming pretty damn real these days as I get ready to start my residency in a few months. Realizing I've been lost in a daydream down memory lane, I jerk my attention to Jenna. She's stopped talking and is smiling at me.

"Sorry, spaced out, what?" I stutter, Jenna laughs and repeats herself.

"I just asked if you wanted to come to the group study tonight, we're going to go over the charting stuff for ICU rounds on Wednesday. We're with Dr. Thompson and they're eight of us." She pulls a look of comedic horror and rolls her eyes. Dr. Thompson is notoriously difficult during rounds. He loves to use public humiliation as a teaching tool, and he *despises* groups trailing along behind him.

"Um, yes, I probably should," I don't want to, but I can't skip out on this study group, it could save my ass on Wednesday. "So, Jenna, do you remember that guy at the bar Saturday night? That big guy...the one I knew from home?" She looks confused for a second at the change of subject, but nods.

"That was him in room 327." I almost whisper the words because I don't want them to be true. *His beautiful eyes.* I blink fast for a second and try to get into professional mode where I can be objective. Jenna gasps.

"Ohmygod, I didn't recognize him until you said something! I wonder what happened? I don't remember much, I was pretty far gone by that part of the night. He wasn't very nice though, was he?" Jenna practically vibrates with curiosity.

"Um, no, he was okay, just...quiet." *Yeah he was kind of a jerk to you Jenna, sorry.* "Anyway, I think I'm going to go back and check on him before group. I'll try not to be late, okay?" Jenna's eyes get speculative in a way I don't like at all.

"Do you want me to come with you? He was Hottie McHot... I wouldn't mind giving him a little TLC," Jenna giggles. *FUCK OFF HE'S MINE! Wow, that seems a little extreme and I'm glad I didn't say that out loud. Mine? What the hell, I must be too tired.*

"Ha, no thanks, paws off missy," I keep my tone light and she smiles knowingly, tapping her lips with one manicured nail.

"Mm-hmm I see," she pats my cheek with a little laugh. "Okay Wren, I'll leave you to your 'friend' from home." She air-quotes 'friend' before picking up her tray. "But I want details, that man is H-O-T. Got it?"

"Oh geez," I mutter with a weak little laugh, "there won't be any details...he's just not into-" *danger, danger, abort, do NOT say princesses.* "I mean I haven't seen him in a long time, there's nothing there, I just want to check in, that's all." It sounds weak, we both know it, but Jenna lets me off the hook. *Oh man, I hope he's not into princesses.*

The Hits Keep Coming

❧

Kane

"-time will tell if his vision has been irreparably damaged." The doctor's words ring through my brain on a loop. I've never felt so helpless in my entire life. Sharp pain brings me back to myself as I realize I'm trying to curl my damaged right hand into a fist. They've got it in some sort of soft wraps that keep me from moving it much, and I try to relax, it doesn't help anything if I hurt it worse.

Blind-sided by an angry drunk. I should know better. I always pay attention as I'm leaving the bar. I'm not going to win any Miss Congeniality contests at this job, and that wasn't the first guy I ever helped make an exit. I'd been thinking about Wren. Wondering if she lived around here somewhere, she'd said med school, that was something. The university hospital was part of a private college, she must be damn smart if she was going there.

Momentarily distracted, I almost miss the knock on the door.

"Yeah," my voice is rough. I wet my lips and wish I knew if there was a glass of water sitting near me. The door clicks open, I hear someone take a few steps into the room, shutting the door behind them. Heels click on the linoleum and a woman clears her throat.

"Mr. Morgan," her voice is crisp, official sounding. "I'm June Nelson from Social Services, I'm in charge of your discharge planning and I have a few questions."

Neighborly, Not Weird

❧

W^{ren}

"Did they figure out what they're going to do with the guy in 327?" My head swivels towards the aides whispering at the nurses station as I walk by, but they don't notice me.

"No, but it sounds like he doesn't have anyone, no wife or family, and they're looking to get him out of here because he doesn't have insurance either." One giggles quietly. "I'd take him home, that's a whole lot of *man* right there." They sigh together and start talking about the gallbladder in 303.

Doesn't have anyone…no insurance…walking to his room, I hesitate outside. *What am I doing? I'm just checking in, we're both a long way from home and he's all alone. This is neighborly, not weird. Neighborly. Not. Weird.* Giving a quick knock, I hear a grunt of some sort, take it for a 'Come In' and open the door.

Kane is sitting in an armchair by the window of his room,

his face tilted toward the sun. They've taken off most of the bandaging, but I can see the tape along his lash lines, keeping them shut. He's got a line of sutures through his left eyebrow and another set along the lid, tiny little knots in some areas, glue on others. There are a lot of superficial scratches and a huge bruise covers the left side of his eye socket and cheekbone.

His arm is propped on a pillow and he's wearing a gray t-shirt and scrub pants. The shirt sleeves strain to fit his arms, and the scrubs are having similar difficulty with his thighs. Walking in, I stare at him as I shut the door behind me, four years haven't changed a thing. He's still the man that held my hand and spun me dizzy on that dance floor. All those muscles and all that power, and he held me like I was a butterfly. I wish he would have held me tighter. *I wish I'd gone to the dance on his arm that night.*

"You a nurse?" Kane mutters, jerking me right out of lalaland, "I don't need any pain stuff yet." He turns his face in my direction, jaw tight.

"Hi Kane, it's Wren." I quickly whisper the words before I let the pause get too long and weird.

"Wren?"

"Yeah, it's me, remember I told you I was in med school? We did rounds through here this morning, I couldn't believe my eyes when we walked into this room and you were laying there, Kane." Stepping further into the room, I walk over to the window and sit in the folding chair facing him, our knees a couple of feet apart.

"What happened to you?" I breathe, reaching out one hand to touch his, he tenses up for a second and I pull my hand away, not meaning to startle him. He lets out a tiny sigh and then slowly turns his hand over, palm up. Reaching out again, I lay my hand in his carefully and his fingers close over mine. *Why is my damn heart racing?*

"I kicked a jackass out of the bar for fighting and he came back and waited out back until I locked up. Blindsided me with a bottle...literally." Kane grunts out a pained laugh at the unintended pun. His next words surprise me.

"I wish I could see you, Wren." His voice is tight, afraid.

"I wish you could too, but I would have needed a hair brush before I came in if you could," I try to keep my tone light, I can't even imagine what he's going through, he rewards me with a tiny smile.

"I'm doing clinicals here for a few more days. Then I get a break while I wait for my residency match." I squeeze his hand lightly. "I talked to the doctor a little more at the end of rounds, she'll be in again tomorrow. They're just keeping your muscles relaxed and your eyes closed while they heal." I squeeze his hand again.

"How long until they let me open my eyes?" His voice is lower than usual, nervous.

"It's going to be a couple days, maybe more on the left, but they'll stop relaxing the muscles tomorrow, too long can cause nerve damage." I can tell he was hoping for sooner, his shoulders bunch up and he frowns, a worry line appearing between his eyebrows that I want to smooth away.

"I can't stay here, Wren. My insurance is shit and I'll go crazy...I'll be fine at my place."

"Where do you live?" As soon as the question leaves my lips, Kane snorts lightly.

"I've got a place about a mile from the bar." He sets his jaw stubbornly.

"So you'll be on your own?" My voice sounds small to me,

I don't want to say that to him, I feel like I'm projecting my own fear into the question. I'd be scared to death if I had to go home all alone and try to figure everything out, blind.

"I'm used to being alone." He slides his hand away from mine, and his voice is hard, but somewhere I find the courage to respond anyway.

"You don't have to be alone. I'll help you."

She Remembered

K^{ane}

"I don't need help." I'm angry. Angry at everything. That stupid drunk and his bottle, my old man for being such a pile-of-shit, Wren for seeing me at my worst. I don't even feel like a fucking man right now, sitting here in pajama pants with my fucking eyes taped shut.

"I think you do." Her voice is quiet and firm, but she's not angry. "I know this is hard, and it's awful, there's no two ways about that, Kane, but you're going to need some help," she pauses before adding, "and I want to," very softly.

My heart squeezes in my chest and I want her to say it again so I know I heard her right, but it hurts too much to admit how helpless I feel. My pride takes over and I turn my face away from where I believe she's sitting.

"All I need is a pass out of this hospital and a ride home." *That's not all I need.*

"Well, we'll start there, the doctor will be through in the morning to see how you're doing. They're going to do x-rays on your hand, hopefully they don't find a fracture. If it is a break, you can get your cast on tomorrow, they're waiting for the swelling in your hand to go down enough." She pauses and sucks in a breath. "I just figured tonight I'd check in, see if you needed anything…maybe keep you company."

Her voice is trying to be brave, but a tiny tremor runs through it and I don't know why. Is it because the doctor isn't going to think my eyes are healing and she's nervous? Or because she's wondering if I want her here? *I do, I want her to stay, I want her to tell me my face isn't ripped up and my eyes will be fine.*

"I'm tired, you don't have to stay." My pride is an asshole that won't shut up. Wren doesn't respond. Standing up carefully, I ignore her little intake of breath as I reach for the bed rail I know is a couple feet to my left. Finding it, I sit on the edge of the bed and then lay down, pulling a pillow under my wrapped arm to support it as I turn partly on my side away from her.

A moment later, I feel the bed sag a tiny bit behind my back as Wren sits on the edge. Her hand touches my shoulder and starts to lightly trail back and forth over my shoulder blade, up to my neck, stroking, her nails light as a feather as they tickle up the back of my neck and into my hair. Soothing me like a wounded animal. I don't have any fight left today, and my pride is finally silent. I let myself relax and hear her hum a few notes before she starts singing softly.

Give me a word,
  give me a sign,
  show me where to look,
  tell me what will I find…

Heat blooms in my chest and I reach back for her hand. She fumbles the words for just a moment when I gently kiss her knuckle and tuck her hand against my chest. I'm so tired. I need her. *She remembered the song.*

She keeps singing softly, resting against my back, and sleep takes me.

I wake up alone later. I can tell the room is dark but I don't have any idea how much time has passed. Sitting up, I feel around and manage to knock something off the little table that's hovering over my knees. Someone must have heard the noise because there's a quick knock and the door opens.

"Can I help you with anything?" I recognize the voice of a nurse that was in earlier.

"Yeah, something's on the floor and did the blonde woman that was here earlier leave?" I hear a little laugh as the nurse moves around the room.

"I've got it hon- no problem," her voice is friendly, whatever I dumped must not have made a mess. "Yes, Wren had to get to a meeting, but she left a message for you." The nurse lays her hand on my shoulder and presses something cool into my hand. A phone. "She told us to let you know that she set up voice commands on your phone and programmed her number into it. She'll be back in to see you tomorrow."

No Time for L-U-V

W^{ren}

Waking up the next morning, I feel like my eyes are full of sand. It took me a long time to fall asleep last night. I was thinking of Kane…that tiny kiss. How every muscle in my body tightened up in the most delicious way when he pulled my hand in close to his chest. How it felt to lean against his broad back and feel him relax while I sang that song.

I don't even know what made me sing, but that song has been playing on a loop in my head since I saw him in that bar a couple of days ago. It was our one slow dance, interrupted too soon. It's crazy how you meet someone, just for a little while, but that tiny part of your life starts to feel so important. *He* feels important. Four years feels like it was four days, and I just want to pick up where we left off as if time stood still. *I want that dance.*

But Kane's hurt. Not just his eyes, which alone would be enough, I felt all the strain bleed out of him last night, just for a little while. Something isn't right, and I can't figure out why Kane is even here, working at a random bar. When he left Gravity, he called his boss, said he had a family emergency, so where's his family? The night was long, and thinking my way through all the questions in my head answered none of them.

Plus I'm graduating and starting my residency this fall…a relationship is a complication I probably don't need right now. *My heart disagrees… vehemently…* I'll see him later. Shaking my head at myself in the mirror, I pull up my hair carefully and quickly take stock. Ready to go, I grab my coffee and head for the hospital. Time to get rounds with Dr. Thompson over with, *hopefully embarrassment free.*

* * *

Three hours later, I feel like I've been run over by a bus, but it's over. The size of the group really set Thompson off, but I answered everything he shot at me in his clipped tones satisfactorily enough to avoid being ridiculed.

Jenna wasn't as lucky, and I catch up to her in the cafeteria as she's fuming over a mug of steaming hot tea.

"I thought his use of 'nimrod' was a little much." I offer.

"Now, get it right Wren, my new title is 'Grade-A Nimrod'," Jenna responds with a wry smile, and then she huffs out a sigh. "I swear, he was really on a roll today, all I could do was think, 'don't cry, don't cry, don't cry' in my head over and over." She blurts out a little laugh, "I also pictured several macabre ways for him to perish and almost cracked a smile right in his face…

that would have been a disaster."

"Maybe next time do the trick public speaking teachers talk about and just picture him in his underwear." I laugh, and then we're both picturing portly little Dr. Thompson in his tighty-whities and laughing too hard to speak. The stress of the morning fades, it's just another day, we made it through.

"So how's Kane?" Jenna asks, still giggling softly as she wipes a tear away.

"Well, possibly blind, possibly proud owner of a broken arm, probably unemployed…" I shrug, spreading my hands on the table to ground myself. "He's alone, and he's hurt, and he's angry…and stubborn." I smile, reliving the conversation last night that was going all wrong until, all of a sudden, it went *right.* "But we're going to be okay, HE'S, *he's* going to be okay." I glance at Jenna and her smile is amused.

"I think 'we're' is more accurate. *Somebody* is in L-U-V," she teases with a smile. "If I can do anything to help, let me know, but I'd say he's lucky you two ran into each other again, might be a tiny bit of *fate* even." She wiggles her fingers in what's probably supposed to be a mystical fashion and stands up, picking up her mug.

"I'll see you later Wren." Jenna walks out of the cafeteria, leaving me staring bemusedly into a bowl of cooling soup. *L-U-V. I don't have time for L-U-V…that is a terrible idea.* Shoveling the soup in my mouth before it gets any colder, I take my tray back and tell myself to go catch a nap while I can. I've got a long night in the ER ahead of me.

Never one to listen, I head back upstairs to room 327. Kane isn't there, but his phone is still on the table and his jeans are laying over the back of a chair. I'm relieved he didn't just try to leave, I'm guessing he's at x-ray or, *hopefully not*, getting a cast on his arm. Sinking into the recliner in the corner, I rest my eyes for just a second.

Cabin Fever and a Cat Nap

❧

Kane

I flex my fingers cautiously, rewarded by a stinging pain flashing across my knuckles. It's not broken, no cast, just some kind of ace wrap to support it some because the brace didn't fit right. That flustered the doctor a little bit, it was the biggest one they had, but it doesn't matter, as soon as I'm out of here I won't wear it anyway. I just wish they'd let me open my eyes.

"They're not ready yet," the doctor's voice is kind when I ask. "The eye heals fast, and we're going to stop the muscle relaxer this afternoon, but you're going to have to be patient. Your ophthalmologist will be checking in tomorrow." I hear scribbling as if the doctor is making a note while I wrap my head around that last word.

"Tomorrow? Doc, I'm going home this afternoon." I am going to crawl right out of my skin if I don't get out of this

43

hospital. I don't know where anything is and everything smells weird and it's so damn noisy. So many things in this place *beep*.

"This afternoon? That's not going to be possible Kane. Just bear with us a few more days. Let me get your surgeon in to take a look at your eyes…do you have someone to stay with you at home for now?" That last sounds cautious, the doctor and the discharge planner have obviously been talking. My lack of 'a healthy support system to assist me in healing' as June kept referring to what I assume would be solved by a wife, or a girlfriend, or a friend, or a family member that cared, really threw her into a tizzy.

"Yeah, I know Doc, I'm lacking in the 'support system' department. I've got a friend who's going to help me." It feels weird to refer to Wren as a friend. I don't know what she is, 'friend' fits, it just doesn't feel like enough. Maybe it should be capitalized, like a title. *The hell? Obviously I have a concussion too. Honestly, maybe friend is too much, she barely knows me.*

It hurts to admit that, even in my head. I'm all in with this girl, *for no good reason other than love at first sight works on me apparently. 'Love at first sight', that's ironic.* She might just be a really nice person. That's probably exactly the case, we had a dance and a laugh and she's just a nice Southern girl looking in on someone she knew from home. She's going to be a *doctor* for fuckssake, she must like helping people. She probably looks at me and sees a big guy covered in ink who bounces at a shit bar. A dumbass who got busted up in an alley because he got distracted and forgot to pay attention.

But she remembered the song…

"I'm glad to hear that." The doctor's voice interrupts my internal pity-party. "You can tell your friend you'll be ready to go home at the end of the week. Get some rest, Mr. Morgan."

An aide turns my wheelchair and we're heading down the hall before I can argue any more. One more night.

"Kane? There's a blonde lady asleep in your room, do you want me to wake her up?" The aide's voice is young, breathy. We've stopped out in the hall, she must have seen Wren through a window or something.

"No, let her sleep, where's she at?" That'd be my luck, I'd go in trying to let her take a nap and sit on her.

"She's in the recliner in the corner, she's just curled up in it, she didn't put the foot part up." The aide must find this romantic or something. She's whispering and I'd swear she's smiling. Pushing up from the arms of the wheelchair, my hand twinges again as I stand.

"I'll just walk in from here, get me through the door." The aide doesn't say anything, but she takes my elbow as I stand up and leads me into the room. We walk in about ten feet and she pulls on my arm a little, leading my hand to the bed. I nod and she pats my shoulder. I feel her move away from me, the door closing quietly as she leaves.

Sitting on the edge of the bed carefully, I smile as I hear a light snore from the corner. Swinging my legs up into bed, I lean back and listen to her sleeping.

I might have fallen asleep too, but it only feels like a few minutes later when I hear a tinkly little alarm sound from near the window. Wren sucks in a breath as she wakes up and fumbles around, silencing her phone.

"I don't know what time it is, but this feels like a random time of day for an alarm," I say quietly to let her know I'm awake.

"Oh, sorry!" Her voice is flustered. "You caught me sleeping, I came to see how you were and I've got a shift in the ER tonight."

"I'm glad you got a nap," I grumble, uncomfortable that she's putting herself out for me. "No cast," I lift up my hand and wiggle the fingers a little, "my hand will be okay, it's just a bad sprain." It's hard to keep the disappointment out of my voice as I keep talking. I feel so damn helpless. "They're making me stay a while yet, I've got to see the eye surgeon who worked on me in the morning I guess."

"I've been thinking about when you get discharged from the hospital," Wren's voice is calm, and I can tell she's probably got a determined look on her face.

"You said your place is near the bar, and that's at least 40 minutes from here," she says carefully. "I've got an apartment three minutes from the hospital, and they'll probably need you in for follow up visits for your eyes, plus some physical therapy to make sure your hand heals well," she's talking faster now. "I think you should come and stay with me for a while." The words come out in a rush and then it's silent for a moment and I realize she's waiting for me to speak.

I Dub Thee Snake and Brick

W^{ren}

So Kane is coming home with me. Yeah, that's happening, and all of a sudden I'm so nervous I don't know what to do. He argued a little bit, but it seemed pretty obvious that this is the best choice. He argued, I countered, he argued a little more, I heartlessly asked him if he wanted to call someone else.

He gave in, and then grumped a little bit more. I just stared shamelessly at the muscles bunching in his shoulders while he sat up and swung his legs over the side of the bed.

"I'm going to need your address so I can get you some things from your place." It would be embarrassing if he could see me right now, I'm twisting my hands, all my professional training is out the damn window, I'm blushing like a teenager and my voice sounds funny. *I'm going to bring 6'5" and 275 pounds of solid muscle, tattoos and bearded goodness to my apartment. Yes, I took a peek in his chart.*

"Okay," he sighs, resigned. It's not the most enthusiastic response, but I understand that he doesn't want to put me out. I haven't even told him that I live in a one bedroom apartment. *My couch is pretty comfy, we'll get by just fine.*

Gathering my bag and checking my hair in the mirror, I get ready to head in for my ER shift. He's still sitting on the edge of the bed, face turned toward me, and my heart clenches. *This is not L-U-V. I would do this for any of my friends. I'm going to be a doctor, I'm supposed to help people. This is NOT L-U-V.*

"It's going to be okay, Kane." Walking back to him, I rest my hand on his shoulder, taking as much comfort from his warmth and strength as I hope he's getting from me.

"It'll have to be, come what may," he says softly.

"Come what may," I agree and walk out the door.

* * *

My shift at the hospital seems extra long today. There was a scheduling mix-up and instead of Jenna, my usual partner, I'm stuck with Bradley. *"Don't call me 'Brad' Wren, it's so uncouth"*. Bradley is good with patients and efficient. The problem with Bradley is that we tried to date briefly, our final disastrous date was about three weeks ago, and he's not as sure as I am that we're actually done.

"Shall we get a beer, Love?"

I'm stunned into silence for a moment as I hand my notes to the charge nurse. Turning to him, I'm wondering if possibly I've been *too* nice. I tried to let him down easy, but, seriously... enough.

"No, and don't call me Love. We went on four dates, it didn't work out. We can be friends but only if you stop acting like we are still dating." Looking into his boyish face with cute brown eyes and that dimple in his chin, I don't think he's going to be able to accept friendship.

"Oh, Wrenny-penny we just needed to slow things down a bit," I bristle because his tone is really condescending, *Wrenny-penny?!* "I know you got all worried about fitting a relationship in with clinicals, but they're almost over. Lighten up."

I never should have told him I didn't have time to date him. I should have told him I didn't *want* to date him. Time to rip it off like a bandaid.

"I wasn't worried, I was letting you down easy. I don't want to date you Bradley. I'm sorry to hurt your feelings." Turning, I walk away quickly, not looking back as I push open the door to the changing rooms. Exhausted, I change and head for my car, Bradley's BMW isn't in the lot, hopefully he got the message for real this time.

Deciding to go back to my apartment, I grab a few hours' sleep. Feeling refreshed, I shower and take a look around. Trying to guess what would make things easier for Kane, I rearrange a little bit, and change the sheets. Cleaning up as I go, I give Max an ear scratch. He stares at me with big gold eyes before yawning and tucking his black head into his paws, ignoring me as only a cat can. I found him out by the dumpster in the parking lot about a month ago. I left him food for a couple days and never saw his mother or any other kittens. Finally I brought him inside, and we've developed an understanding. *Mostly that I feed him and he occasionally head butts me at three a.m. when he wants attention, but...it's a work in progress.*

Grabbing my bag, I lock the door behind me, plug Kane's address into my phone, and steer my Jetta toward the outskirts of town. I don't know what to expect, but the address has a ½ behind the number, so it's some kind of apartment. Turns out, there's a tiny little main street remaining down the road from Joe's bar. Remnants of all the old businesses stand mostly vacant, but there's a hardware store, a dime store, and a diner still open for business.

Kane's apartment is over the hardware store. Parking in the alley behind the building next to a truck, I see a note on the dashboard with Kane's name visible through the window. The door's unlocked, so I open it and reach inside, taking both the note and the keys that are in the cupholder. Opening the note, I scan it quick.

Kane-

Sorry to hear you're laid up, the police were here, I gave them your number. They picked Kenny up that same night, blind drunk, his hands bleeding all over the place from the bottle he broke. He babbled a lot, admitted everything, he's in the can and it looks like Brenda's going to be single for a while.

I banned the rest of that crew from the bar. Troy is holding things down okay for now, and your job will be here if you still want it when you're better.

-Joe

Tucking the note and keys in my bag, I lock the truck and walk up the rickety back stairs, unlocking the door to Kane's apartment. Entering a dark little hallway, I walk past a door to the right that houses a small laundry, another door that seems to be a closet, and then the hallway opens up into a kitchen.

The kitchen is spotless. I glance in the fridge quick to see if anything needs to be thrown away, but other than some bottled water and a couple of beers, there's nothing in there. There's an island counter dividing the open kitchen from the living area. The front of the apartment has been split into a living room and bedroom, each having two of the building's front windows. The kitchen is lit by a skylight and the light that filters back from the living room windows.

Everything is simple, no pictures on the walls. Grey tweed couch, darker grey recliner pointed at a mid-size TV. Laptop sitting on a coffee table that's seen better days, bookshelf stuffed with books. A small table in front of one window supports a big healthy aloe vera plant, and it makes me smile to think of Kane taking care of something. *I am an emotional idiot, the idea of a guy watering a plant makes my heart go pitter-pat? Wow.* I give the plant a drink and continue wandering around.

Walking into Kane's bedroom, it's more of the same, the bed is made, there's a few clothes in the laundry basket in the corner, a dresser and a nightstand piled high with books. Out of curiosity, I glance through the titles, he seems to read across several types, some mystery, some military, a couple of fantasy in the mix. A dog-eared copy of *The Diamond Throne* catches my eye. I've never read it, and it seems to be well-loved, so I tuck it in my bag.

There's one small framed picture on the dresser, I walk over and pick it up. It's a much younger Kane, in boxing shorts, gloves up, flexing, with a prize belt around his waist. A man that has to be his father stands next to him, smiling. Setting it gently back on the dresser, I wonder what happened, how he went from boxing to bouncing in a bar with no friends or family around.

Opening the closet, I see a duffle bag on the shelf and pull it out. Setting it on the bed, I start getting the essentials out of the closet and dresser. *A little prayer of thanks went up when I saw that he owns three pairs of grey sweatpants...*

Moving to the bathroom, there's a small bag in the drawer. I drop in his toothbrush, shampoo and some beard stuff that's sitting on the counter. It seems reasonable to pack enough for a week. I try not to think too hard about what happens if a week passes and he still can't see. *No sense worrying about what hasn't happened yet...come what may, he said.*

Taking a last look around, I toss a phone charger in the bag, zip it up and shoulder it, walking back through the apartment turning off lights as I go. There's a little row of hooks on the side of the kitchen cabinet, keys hanging on two of them. One appears to be a spare set of truck keys. The other has a little tag that says 'Box 3' hanging with a small key that looks like it probably goes to a mailbox. I take the little key and walk out the door, locking it carefully behind me.

Stowing Kane's duffle in the backseat of my car, I wander around the side of the building, looking for a mailbox. Up near the street, there's a little side entry to the building with a grimy window covered in flyers facing the street, a pay phone *I didn't even know those existed anymore,* and several mailboxes built into the wall. The key fits the third box. Grabbing the small pile of mail, I sift out the junk, tossing a couple of flyers and furniture sale notices in a nearby bin.

The bell jingles on the door of the diner and I hear voices. It sounds like two men grumbling to each other about non-smoking laws being annoying. Glancing out the window to the street, I see two men in their fifties, flannel shirts, dirty boots, lighting up cigarettes as the waitress follows them out.

"If it's the guy you're looking for, I think he lives up there," the waitress points to the left, up at Kane's apartment. I freeze in the middle of stuffing the mail in my bag and listen hard. They can't see me from where they're standing while I'm in this little nook.

"You seen 'im today?" One of the men asks the waitress.

"No, but I usually only see him for lunch, he's pretty quiet." Her voice is nervous. She doesn't like these men. I don't either, so I stay out of sight.

"If'n he shows up, you call this number, hear? I'll gi' ya fifty bucks." The second man's voice is low and mean.

"O-o-okay," the waitress stammers and I hear the bell jingle again as she quickly escapes into the diner.

"Think he's here?" The first man I'm going to call Brick because he looks dumb and mean. The second man I've dubbed Snake because he's got slicked back greasy hair and narrow eyes.

"Let's ask the guy in here if'n he's got a key since it's his store. If Kane's not home we can see if he's got it first, I don't really want to try to look with him in there." Snake takes a big drag on his cigarette, tossing it aside.

"Ask?" Brick smiles.

"Yeh, just *ask* you asshole, we can always bust the damn door, no sense someone callin' the cops 'cause you pounded some store clerk." Snake sneers and Brick grimaces, disappointed.

I hear them enter the hardware store and make the quick decision to test the payphone. Dialing 911, I wait to hear the operator answer and whisper, "Someone is trying to break into the apartment." I give Kane's address and drop the phone. I quickly jog back up the side of the building to my car before they get done 'talking' to the poor clerk in the hardware store. *Hopefully that keeps the clerk in one piece and Kane's apartment from getting trashed.*

I don't waste any time, tossing my bag in the passenger seat, I drive the opposite way down the back alley, not wanting them to see me or my car. *Why are they looking for Kane, and what else are they trying to find?*

Accidental Strip Tease

─•◦◯◦•─

K^{ane}

"I'm going to let you open your right eye Mr. Morgan."

I feel cool fingers peeling away tape and a cotton swab with something cold and wet runs along my eyelashes. "You had a corneal laceration, but the piece of glass that was in your eye when you arrived was removed and everything seems to be healing without signs of infection." More cold, wet swabbing along my lashes.

"Now?" I want to be able to see, I want this to have been two terrible days that end with my eye working.

"Go ahead, we've dimmed the lights, you'll have a lot of sensitivity." The doctor hesitates, then adds, "don't be disappointed if you only have shadows and blurriness initially, that's common and should continue to improve over the next week." My heart sinks, but anything would be better than it is now.

Fluttering my lashes open, I squint even against the dim light in the room. Shadows, black and grey, I can see the light on the walls and through the window of the door, but it's all shadows.

"Your left eye is more severe, you've had two deep corneal lacerations as well as blunt trauma to the iris. We've kept it closed except for applying antibiotics to avoid your eyelid rubbing too much, as well as to allow the cuts on your eyelid to heal with minimal scarring. One of them went through your lash line and those sutures will be in a while."

"What does all of that mean Doc?" I need him to speak plain English.

"That means that I'm going to put an antibiotic mesh in your left eye, it's similar to a contact lens. I'm going to have you wear a shield over it to avoid the possibility of any further injury. We'll take the lens out in a week and see how your vision is progressing." I hear clicking as the doctor types something into the computer. I keep hoping my eye will just start working, but it's still all shadows.

"A shield...like an eye patch?" *I am going to look like a damn pirate.*

"No Mr. Morgan," the doctor sounds amused. "This is a clear plastic lens with air-holes, you'll keep it taped over the eye, but you don't have to keep your eyes closed anymore. At this point you need time to heal and we have to keep you from getting an infection." A nurse walks into the room and the doctor reclines my chair, Q&A is over.

* * *

Some time later, an aide is wheeling me back to my room and I'm slowly blinking my eyes behind a pair of dark sunglasses.

I'm pretty sure my grandpa had a pair of these. I can wear these during the day and I have to tape these stupid plastic pieces over my eyes while I sleep. *Bet Wren doesn't let me get away with skipping those...but I also bet it'd hurt like a bitch to accidentally rub my eyes right about now.*

Wren arrives in the evening after her shift, she tells me about her day and in general keeps the conversation rolling single-handedly. I want them to let me go home.

"They'll let you go as soon as they can, Kane." Wren says patiently when I grump about it for the tenth time in ten minutes.

We fall into a routine and the next couple of days pass pretty quickly. I've got therapy every morning for my hand, and Wren comes in each day when she gets done with her shift. She's excited to be done and on to her residency.

Finally the doctor signs off on my discharge. Wren and I have another discussion about whether or not I should come to her apartment or go home to my own. She wins.

"Do you need help getting ready to go?" The nurse has put in my drops and checked everything over, and now an aide has arrived to help me.

"Yeah, I'm going to shower quick and if you could put all my clothes on the bed I can get changed." I'm not even sure what I have here. "I guess if there's any extra stuff put it in a bag or something. Wren will be here soon."

"Sure thing, Kane." I hear her bustling around the room, cabinets and drawers open and close. She pats me on the shoulder.

"Ok, I've got your clothes and stuff ready, I can take you in and get the water going." She sounds like she's older, so this is a little less weird, the aide that came in yesterday and offered to help me get dressed sounded like she was a teenager and couldn't stop giggling. I kicked her out *nicely* and managed to put my shirt on both inside out *and* backwards.

"Thanks." Standing I start walking towards the light shining from the bathroom door. She takes my elbow when I get close.

"You've probably got this memorized by now, but left is hotter, right is colder and off. Soap and washcloth to the right on a shelf about hip high on you. Don't let the water spray in your eyes, but a few drops won't hurt anything. Towels right here." She guides my hand to the towels and then to the grab bar by the shower.

"Do you need help or privacy sir?" I can hear the smile in her voice, and I like her even more for being cool.

"I'm good, I think, just tell me when I come out if I put anything on backwards."

"You got it, I'll be back in 20 minutes." She laughs and I nod. Turning toward the shower I pull my shirt over my head. I hear a little gasp and she whispers, "Ho-ly Moses," under her breath. I can feel my neck getting red and I don't know which way to turn to stop giving her a show.

"Sorry."

"Oh Hon, I'm sorry for being a ninny, you'd think I was one of those young'uns, but well, now I feel like I should thank you for the art display." She laughs, "and now that I've embarrassed both of us, I'm actually going to leave. Back in 20, I'll knock." I wait until I hear her footsteps and she closes the door louder than usual.

When she comes back, I'm sitting on the bed and I feel human again. My shirt is on right and my jeans zipped up the front. *It's the little things right now.*

"Okay sir, here's the paperwork for Wren-, well speak of the devil, hey Wren, he's all ready for you. Here's the scripts to pick up, he's got a couple kinds of drops and some pain pills." I can see her shadow move into the room and I'm nervous all of a sudden.

"Hey Kane, hey Louise." She comes up close and puts a hand on my shoulder. Leaning in, I can tell she's looking at my face, and I wish more than anything that I could see hers right now.

"Everything looks good, Kane, it's so nice to see the bandages off." She steps back and I hear her stuffing the paperwork in her purse.

"Yeah, feels good, wish I could see more than shadows."

"It'll come," her voice is soft, less certain. I stand up from the bed, feeling too vulnerable. She takes my hand and lays it on her shoulder, leading me.

"Your chariot awaits."

Reluctant Houseguest

❦

*W*ren

Kane's kind of big for a Jetta.

He's also not very chatty, but that's nothing new. Before I pull out of the lot, I realize I didn't tell him about my trip to his place.

"Hey, something weird happened when I went to get your stuff." *I wonder if the cops arrived in time to scare those guys off.*

"What kind of weird." His tone is guarded.

"I went down and found your mailbox, and while I was there I saw two guys and a waitress from the diner come outside and they were talking about finding someone and she pointed at your apartment." I pause, but he doesn't respond and he's very still beside me.

"Anyway, I probably could have talked to them, but they looked sketchy and were talking about looking for something and roughing up the hardware store clerk...so I called 911 from the payphone and bailed." *And now that sounds like overkill and I feel stupid.*

"You called 911?" He actually grins for just a second.

"Yeah…it kind of feels like overkill now…but the payphone was there and I didn't know what to do." I get a fluttery nervous feeling in my belly as I park and walk around the car to meet him. Taking his hand, I put it on my shoulder again and lead him inside.

"That was a good idea. I don't know who they were." He clams up at that point, his face is tense and closed off.

"Come on, it's just my apartment." I try to joke him into a little smile, "You look like I'm leading you to the electric chair." He grunts softly and I glance back to catch his face softening just a little.

"I know, I just…" he sighs, "this is a lot to ask of you."

"Oh, well, you know, us southern girls and our hospitality," I laugh lightly. "Really, it's *fine*. I've got a couple more days to finish this clinical rotation and then the match ceremony next week. After that, I'm on break until my residency starts." I wish I knew where I was going already, this is the culmination of four hard years.

"Match ceremony?"

"Yeah, you know, doctors are *super* busy, no time to date, so they do a great big group date and marry us all off quick." I snort out a little laugh at my own *dumb* joke.

"Um…"

"I'm kidding, the match is where we all get our letters and find out where we're going to do our residencies, it's a big day."

"Dr. Donovan sounds good, Wren. That's a lot of hard work." *I know he's just being nice, but I want him to say Dr. Donovan again in his growly man-voice reallll bad.*

61

"Dr. Donovan does sound good. Really good. Med school has been the hardest thing I've ever done. The first couple years I wasn't sure I was cut out for it, but here I am." I hear myself sigh happily and realize I'm rambling.

"Anyway, here's my apartment," I unlock the door and lead him into the living room. "The entire thing is in one long row, the wall that connects to the apartment behind is on the right, so we're in the living room, kitchen is next, then a hall with a bedroom and the bathroom is at the end." His hand is warm on my shoulder as I lead him in, I have the insane urge to lead him to the couch for a cuddle. *He's not interested. He can't see for fuckssake, I'm not going to be the pervy weirdo that hits on him while he's healing.*

"Mmrrowlll?" My awkward little moment of self doubt is interrupted by Max as he stretches and stands up from the couch, stalking closer to investigate the new intruder to his domain.

"It's probably a little late in the game to ask, but you're not allergic to cats are you?" I turn to look at him.

"No, I'm just glad that's a cat, I thought it was your stomach and I had concerns." He feels the cat's head bump against his fingers and scratches him behind the ear.

I blurt out a laugh and turn again, leading him around the end of the sectional that sticks out into the room.

"So I figured you could rest here in the living room, or do you want to go to bed?" *Ohmygod.* "I mean sleep. Just you. Sleeping or sitting." *Ohmygod I can't shut up.* "I mean…are you tired or would you rather watch TV or something?" *OHMYGOD I CAN'T SHUT UP, TV!?* "God, I'm sorry, TV was a stupid thing to suggest." I finally just seal my lips shut and silently die a slow, painful, death. Kane hasn't said a word, but his hand moves a little, and I glance over my shoulder to see him shaking his head as he smiles.

"Sitting is fine, and I can listen to the TV, it's okay, Wren." *And now he's comforting me in the midst of my stupidity. Awesome.*

"You hungry? I was just going to order us some takeout, I've got a couple of hours before I've got to be back at the hospital." I finally walk forward and steer his hand to the arm of the couch. He lets go of my shoulder with a friendly squeeze that makes me blush and sits down with a sigh.

"Yeah that's good, what kind of food?" he leans back and closes his eyes. Max immediately jumps on the couch beside him, nosing at his hand and investigating, and I'm irrationally jealous and at the same time misty. Because, apparently, nothing pushes my waterworks button faster than a man nurturing *anything*.

First a plant, now my cat, I can't imagine what'd I do if I saw him with a baby. My cat, oh there's a double entendre...and now I'm picturing him with our baby and my ovaries just vibrated. STOP IT WREN WHAT THE FUCK!

"There's a mom-and-pop place just down the street that does great burgers?" I smile when he groans happily, I'm still picturing him holding a baby and melting into a little puddle, but my voice sounds normal and he can't see me blushing.

It makes my heart ache, but even if I thought he'd be down, I can't start anything with Kane right now. *I'm moving in a couple of months. He's obviously got too much to worry about already, and I don't even think he likes me, he just doesn't have any other option right now.*

"Yesss, three and fries." He leans to the side and pulls a wallet out of his pocket, holding the whole thing out to me.

"Oh geez, no that's okay, I don't mind, I could cook too, som-"

"Wren," his voice is hard and his eyebrows draw together. "You don't have to cook for me, and I pay." He gives the wallet an insistent little shake. "Now take this damn thing, it'd ruin the effect if I hand you my license."

"Okay." I take the wallet.

Calling in the order, I disconnect, and my phone immediately buzzes with another incoming call. *Ma?* Walking into the kitchen, I answer.

"Ma? Everything okay? Where's Gran?" I try not to sound worried but she usually forgets which contact I am on the phone.

"Wren? Hello Sweetie. Did you call me?" Her beautifully vague tones come down the line, and I clutch the phone tighter to my ear.

"Hi Ma, no I didn't call, but I'm glad to hear from you. Is everything okay?" *Where is Gran.*

"Everything is fine Sweetie, why wouldn't it be?"

"Oh no reason, what are you doing today Ma?" It's best not to confuse her, I can call Gran.

"Oh Wren! We made the most lovely sugar cookies and I thought of you. Gran went to the store for milk. I just love cookies with milk, don't you?" She sounds so happy and my heart breaks. "Would you like to come over for cookies Wren?"

"That's a tempting offer Ma, but I'm over in Texas, remember? In school?"

"School? Eww! Wren, school is boring and you should come over for cookies. Cookies are more fun than school." She giggles and sets the phone down with a little clunk. I hear her move away, singing to herself. After listening for a minute, she doesn't come back on the line, so I disconnect.

We've All Got History

❦

Kane

Humming a sad little tune, Wren comes back in the room, she must have been in the kitchen while she was on the phone. When she brought me in the room, we kind of did a loop around what must be some kind of L-shaped couch, and now I feel it move slightly as she sits heavily on the other end with a sigh.

"Everything okay?" I wish I could see her face, I'm not good with feelings anyway, but it is ten times worse when I can't see her expression.

"Oh, yeah, that was my mom…she's…not well." Wren heaves a sigh, "I don't want to bore you."

"I'm not bored." I could listen to her talk forever.

"Oh, okay," her tone is lighter. "Well, my mom had a bad accident when I was little. It caused a brain injury. She lives with my Gran, that's who raised me." She doesn't sound upset,

65

this is an old hurt, not too hard to talk about.

"What about your father?" *My mother would've been calling me a Nosey Parker at this point.*

"He caused the accident." Her voice has flattened out, this is a sore subject. *Shit.*

"Sorry, I shouldn't be prying."

"No! It's okay, it was so long ago it doesn't help to be upset anymore, but I haven't seen him since that day. I was only five years old, I don't even really remember him." She lets out a shaky breath. "It's hardest on my Gran, she takes care of my mom and raised me because my dad was her son. She feels guilty every day."

"I remember your house being cheerful." I didn't mean to make her sad. *This is why I don't talk much, talking equals sharing feelings, and then I don't know what to do.*

"My house? Oh, you mean in Gravity, I forgot you were there that one time. Yes, it was tiny, but my Gran keeps a huge flower garden and she always did like bright colors. It was a good place to grow up." We lapse into silence for a moment and then she clears her throat lightly.

"Why did you disappear the day after we met, Kane?" She's come back round to the stuff I don't really want to talk about. *I don't want to tell her my old man's a fucking loser who can't stay out of trouble. I don't want to tell her that I used to be a fighter, and then ended up collecting money and threatening people. I don't want to tell her that I'm trying to stay off the radar of a two-bit heavy who wants his ring back because my old man's a fucking idiot. I really don't want to tell her that the two guys she saw today probably work for him.*

"Family emergency," I grunt, and then a knock at the door saves me. It's the food being delivered. Wren pays the kid and

I hear her moving in the kitchen. After a minute she comes and takes my arm.

"Food's on the table," she sounds better, and I sit in the chair she leads me to. She puts a burger in my hand and tells me what's in front of me, and we eat in silence for a minute.

"Damn good burgers," I don't think I've ever had better.

"Yeah, I order from them a lot, they do all the good stuff, hot beef sandwiches, meatloaf on Thursdays, it's a good thing I walk up to 35,000 steps a day and only usually have time for one meal or I'd be a hippo off their food." She laughs and we keep eating. I hear her take a drink and then she clears her throat lightly.

"So…what kind of emergency?" *Crap, she didn't forget.*

"My old man got into some trouble and I moved back to help him out."

"My turn to be nos-" *Nope, this isn't happening.* I cut her off.

"I'm tired, I think I'll crash for a while." I don't want to sound this cold, but this shit is not her problem.

"Oh, sure, sorry, I'm yakking your ear off. I can show you where the bed is." She's quiet, obviously catching on that I don't want to share. *I do, but this is my problem, not yours Wren, and I won't let it be yours, I'll leave before I let that happen.* I stand and she takes my arm and we start walking when I register what she just said and stop. Her hand leaves my arm with a little jerk.

"What's wrong?"

"I can sleep on the couch." I hear her sigh impatiently.

"No you can't, and don't be stubborn. Neither end of that couch is long enough to fit you."

"I'm not kicking you out of your own bed. Maybe you should just take me back to my place, I can call a cab for doctor visits."

This isn't going to work, I can't do this.

"Oh for fuckssake!!" She surprises me into a laugh, but she's not having it. "I'm serious Kane, what the hell? Just sleep in the damn bed. I don't know if you're aware of this, but you're kind of huge. I'm barely five feet tall. I could sleep in that arm chair if I had to, hell I can lay flat in the damn bath tub!"

She pauses for a second and I hear her breathing. I open my mouth cautiously to apologize or something, but she's not done.

"Also I can tell you don't want to talk about whatever is going on with your dad and those guys I saw at your place, but I'm here. You can tell me. I might even be able to help." This time she seems to be done, and the silence lingers for a long minute. Finally she sighs.

"Come on you big stubborn ox." Taking my arm again, she leads me down a short hall to her bedroom.

Lost in a Dream

❧

W^{ren}

Kane sat on the edge of the bed while I got my scrubs out of the closet. He didn't say a word. I headed for the bathroom to get ready and came back in, not sure what to say.

His jaw is set and he's got too many things weighing him down. I can't help him with that right now, I've got a shift in 20 minutes, I just hope he can get some sleep.

"I've got to go, I left you four sandwiches and a couple bottles of water in the fridge. There's chips and some snacks on the counter. Are you going to be okay?" *I want to crawl in that bed, pull him around me like a blanket and make everything okay.*

"I'll be fine, I'm sorry I was rude." His tone is gruff and he turns his face to me.

"I know you will, and it's okay. You've been through a lot." He grunts softly at the understatement. "I'm your friend, Kane, you can trust me with whatever's going on." *I wish I was more than your friend.* He nods and I don't know what else I can say.

"I'll be back late tonight. I'll bring supper if you're up for it." He nods again.

"Thanks."

* * *

I feel unsettled on the drive to the hospital and I'm throwing my stuff in my locker when Jenna arrives, looking fresh and gorgeous. Sometimes I get jealous when I'm around her, I've never seen anyone more organized and put together. Her dark hair is pulled up in a perfect messy bun, *I never get those right,* she's got just enough makeup on, *I haven't had time to put on mascara in three years,* and her clothes have neither wrinkles, nor black cat hairs clinging to them, *bitch.*

"How's your patient, Wren? You two playing doctor at home yet?" She grins at me as she stows her bag in her locker.

"Ha, right. He's fine but we're just friends, Jenna. No doctor-playing." I smile back. "Ready for next weekend?" Match Day is Friday, we both found out Monday that we'd been matched to programs.

"Oh god am I ever!" She claps her hands together. "I just want to *know*, you know? I'm hoping for Philadelphia or Johns Hopkins, but they're so competitive." She finishes putting her things away and we head out onto the floor.

"What're your top two?" She asks as we head for the nurses station.

"I went for two of the rural ones, they really need coverage here in Texas and I also went for one over in Georgia, near home." It's really a win-win, I love it here and going back to Georgia wouldn't be a punishment either.

It's a rough evening. A pediatric code comes into the ER and for a little while I'm worried that the child isn't going to make it. Finally he stabilizes and I'm relieved to see that he's improving before I leave for the night. Other than that, it's a heavy run of the usual and I'm beyond tired when I drive thru for Mexican take-out on my way home.

Juggling the food and my bag, I let myself in the apartment and drop my bag on the couch, taking the food to the little table in the kitchen.

"Wren?" His voice is rough with sleep and I hear Kane moving around in the bedroom.

"Yes, I'm here, I brought food if you're hungry."

"Yeah, um, give me a sec, I lost my clothes." *Lordhavemercy. Don't giggle, don't giggle.*

"All of them?" *Don't giggle, don't giggle, don't giggle.* Kane laughs.

"No, but I think your damn cat stole my shirt. I've got sweatpants on, can you come look?" His tone makes it obvious that while he already loves the cat, he *hates* asking for help. *Sweatpants...thankyoujesus for the second best option after naked.*

Walking down the hall I turn into the bedroom and do a little swoon, grabbing the door jamb to stop myself from tipping over. Kane is *magnificent.* I mean it was obvious he had an amazing body, clothes don't hide that, but *ohmygod.* He's standing there in gray sweatpants, *swoon,* the ink that was visible climbing his arms continues onto his shoulders and most of his back, *swoon, swoon, swoon.* He hears me and turns, his chest is covered in dark reddish brown curls that narrow to a V and disappear into the waistband of his pants, *I'm dizzy.*

I'm blushing so hard I'm about to pass out, but thankfully my voice is steady.

"Hey, I'm here." Spotting the cat, who has indeed stolen Kane's t-shirt, dragged it part way under the bed, and laid on it, I shoo him off and pick it up.

"You don't want to wear this, it's covered in black fur. Sorry!" *I can smell him. That awesome, just been sleeping, man smell... ohmygod.*

Tossing his shirt at the laundry basket in the corner, I grab his bag which is on the floor by the end of the bed. He must have kicked it off while he was sleeping. *Because, duh, I left it there forgetting that some people take up the whole bed.* Setting the bag on the bed, I pull out a t-shirt and hand it to him.

"Thanks," he mutters, pulling it over his head.

"Of course," I turn, grab his hand, and put it on my shoulder, "let's eat, I got you a dozen tacos." He laughs and follows me to the kitchen.

* * *

"So, I borrowed a book from your apartment, I hope that's okay," I take another bite, waiting to see if Kane's in a talk-y mood tonight.

"Yeah, of course, which one?" He is polishing the tacos off in three bites each, I'm glad I got him a solid dozen.

"It's called The Diamond Throne, it looked like one you've read a few times." Kane lets out a snort of laughter.

"A few," he shakes his head, "I like that series, I first read it in high school, it was fun to escape to a world where knights could do magic...I don't know." He trails off uncomfortably, like he's said too much.

"Oh I'm glad to hear it's a series, I'll have to borrow the next one, I've never read anything like it." *Shut up Wren, small talk is stupid.* I manage to stop myself from filling the silence, and we keep eating. The silence is comfortable. It gives me time to think.

Every little detail I find out about Kane makes me want to get closer to him, and I don't know why, but it's super-hot that he reads for fun. *Gray sweatpants, no shirt, book in hand, lounging on my couch...goodlord...that man is my new favorite daydream.*

When we're finished, I clear the dishes and clean the kitchen quickly. Kane wanders out to the living room and sits on the couch, looking uncomfortable. I grab a couple of beers out of the fridge, crack both open and take one to him. Flipping open my laptop, I start a playlist of old rock songs, and sit in the corner of the couch with a sigh.

"Thanks," Kane grunts, visibly relaxing as the first song plays. He takes a couple of drinks and then shifts so he's facing me.

"So what kind of books do you usually read," he asks, *and I about die of the cuteness.*

"Oh, I like all kinds, but mostly light mysteries and rom-coms, I don't like things too serious." I'm curious to hear what he thinks about that, most people I know think that rom-coms are just silly books with sex.

"I always liked books that took me out of reality for a little while," Kane muses, "my old man was...difficult." He shakes his head and takes a swallow of beer.

"I saw the photo at your apartment, it looks like you guys agreed on boxing at least," it's hard to keep the hope out of my voice, but I want Kane to trust me, and I can tell that whatever is on his mind has to do with his dad.

"That was pretty much it, and it didn't last long," Kane says quietly. Finishing off his beer, he stands up and carefully walks out to the kitchen. I hear him set the bottle on the counter, and he comes back into view.

"I'm pretty beat, I think I'll get some sleep," he reaches down to pet Max who is busily twining around his ankles. "Could you give me one of the painkillers?" Kane looks uncomfortable to be asking.

"Of course, do you have a headache?" I ask, standing quickly and walking over to the table.

"Yeah, I think maybe just all the light and stuff, I'm probably trying too hard to see," he grumps, holding out a hand as I shake one of his pills out of the bottle. Crossing to the sink, I get him a glass of water and hand it to him.

"It's getting late, I think I'll get some sleep too," I wish I hadn't put him in this headspace. He's got enough going on without me prying into his life.

He holds the glass out and I take it, our fingers brushing softly. My heart hurts. I want to hug him.

"Goodnight Wren," he murmurs, turning and walking down the hall, muttering a good-natured curse at Max who manages to trip him up twice.

I hear the bedroom door close softly, and I wish I knew why I feel like crying. *Probably because my cat likes that huge, ink-covered, bearded giant better than me. I prefer that to option B... that I'm falling for him and I want to fix everything, and I can't...*

As I'm curled up on the couch, throwing my confused heart a little pity-party, our song comes on...and it's too much. With a tiny sob, I reach over and shut the laptop. Standing, I grab a blanket out of the coat closet, turn off the lights, curl up on the couch, and stare out the big picture window until sleep takes me.

I'm shaken out of an uneasy dream, and it takes me a second to figure out where I am and who yelled, when I hear Kane's voice again.

"Wren!" I stumble down the hall, opening the bedroom door.

"What? What's wrong Kane?" I look quickly around the room, and by the dim glow of a small night light in the hall, I don't see anything immediately wrong. Walking closer to the bed, I look down at Kane. His eyes are closed, brows drawn tightly together, and he looks upset. I'm also pretty sure he's asleep.

"Safe," he mutters, one of his hands knotting the sheet. He doesn't seem as upset, and I'm not sure what to do. I don't want to wake him up and embarrass him, but I don't want him to be trapped in a bad dream either. *Especially one that seems to involve me.*

As I'm standing there, indecisive, he mutters something that might have been 'lost' and his eyebrows knot up again. Without thinking, I reach out and smooth his hair back, trying to soothe him without waking him up.

It backfires spectacularly.

Kane's huge hand closes over my wrist and he pulls me into him, hard. I sprawl onto the bed with a *serious* lack of grace, face-planting into his chest. His arm wraps around my waist, pulling me in tight.

"Baby, I thought I'd lost you," his voice rumbles right into my ear through his chest. With one hand on my ass and one hand behind my neck, Kane slides me up the bed until our faces are level and he's kissing me. *Ohmygod, ohmygod, ohmygod. I should wake him up. He wouldn't do this if he was awake. Well...he might. Would I let him? Yes. Yes I would. Ohmygod, he is so fucking good*

75

at this, maybe just a little bit longer. Wren, you're an asshole! He is asleep! Ohhhh, but he is so good at this, ohmygod, ohmygod.

Kane starts to push me over onto my back, still kissing me, and my conscience finally wins when his hand starts to slide under my shirt. He's rock hard against my hip and he's only wearing underwear to sleep in. *I have to stop him before we reach a point where we both have a cardiac event when he wakes up.*

Grabbing his hand before he gets anywhere interesting, I put my other hand against his chest and push away.

"Kane, wake up," I gasp, *sounding super un-sexy, dammit.* His hands freeze like I stopped time and he pushes up onto an elbow. His expression is completely disoriented and I see his eyes fly open.

"Wren…wha…what's wrong?" His hips shift away and his hand reaches for me, touching my cheek carefully.

"Well, um, you had a…bad dream…I think," *Wow, I'm coming at this all wrong.* "I was a little surprised when you pulled me into the bed." I whisper softly, not sure whether to laugh, kiss him again, or just die of embarrassment.

"I pulled yo-…sorry…did I…say anything?" I'm feeling vulnerable, flat on my back with him still very close, and I scoot away a little and roll on my side, facing him.

"You said my name once," I admit quietly. Kane lays back down on his back, next to me, *sadly not touching me anymore.* His eyes are closed.

"When I was a kid, my mom told me I used to have whole conversations in my sleep," Kane says softly. "I used to sleep walk too." He laughs lightly. "Spent a night in the yard ten feet up a tree once. Almost fell out when I woke up. I think I was eight." I blurt out a startled giggle and he laughs with me. When we fall silent again, I reach out and touch his shoulder.

"I'll let you sleep now," I whisper, sitting up on the edge of the bed.

"Goodnight, Wren," he rumbles, and I almost swoon right back into bed with him. Instead, I stand up and walk back down the hall, where I find Max curled up in my couch spot. He grudgingly lets me slide him over. I fall asleep to Max purring and dream of Kane.

Bless That Damn Cat

*K*ane

Wren's warm hand holds my face still, I try not to blink too much while she puts drops in my eyes. *I woke up kissing Wren last night.*

"Did you put those shields on last night?" Wren murmurs, wiping a stray drop off my temple before it reaches my hair. *I woke up kissing Wren, dick hard enough to piss diamonds, pressed against her hip.*

"Sure," I grunt, not really wanting to talk about those damn things I'm not going to wear. *I'm also not doing any more therapy for my hand, it's fine.*

"Is your right eye getting any clearer?" Her hand moves a tiny bit, a finger running over my cheekbone lightly. We're politely not talking about last night, and I hate it. That was the clearest case of 'ice broken' ever, and I want to take advantage of it. *I want to lean in, I want to put my arms around her and pull*

78

her in close. I wish I had asked her to stay last night.

"Some." Not enough, still shadows and light, no details.

"That's good, it's early yet," her voice is warm, and she pats my shoulder, turning, presumably to put the drops on the table next to us. I hear a yowl from the cat, she must have stepped on him when she turned, she leans into my shoulder heavily as she loses her balance.

"Shit!" She squeaks and sways hard trying to find her footing. The cat runs over my foot and down the hall with a hiss. My hands slide around Wren's waist to steady her and I set her on my knee. Her hand grips my arm tight as she lets out a little gasp. I can feel her breath on my face.

"My hero," she breathes, with a little laugh, "stupid cat underfoot." Her legs shift as if she's going to stand up, and in spite of myself I tense up, wanting to hold her for just a second longer. She freezes, and then, ever so slowly, her weight settles back onto my leg, one of her hands leaves my arm and I feel a feather-light touch on my jaw before her fingers wind into my hair.

"This is probably a bad idea," she whispers.

"Find out," I whisper the dare, not moving a muscle. *I have dreamed about this woman for four stupidly-long years.* She's still for a long moment and I let my eyes close.

Wren's lips are soft as she stretches up and presses them to mine. Her body turns and I relax my arms, letting my hands rest lightly on her hips. She winds her other hand in my hair, tugging lightly as she brings her knees up onto my thighs. She's taller than I am now, kneeling on my lap, and I hold her hips steady as I tilt my head back and let her set the pace.

"I love bad ideas," she gasps, her lips mashing to mine, parting as I feel her tongue flick my lip. Holding her tighter, I kiss her back, tasting cherry lip gloss and orange juice. Breaking the kiss to breathe, I bury my face in her neck, nipping that sweet spot at her collar bone. Kissing my way lower, along the neckline of her shirt, she sighs her pleasure as I squeeze her tight and lay a kiss between her breasts. She's so small, my arms are crossed behind her, my hands on the curve of her ass.

I tilt my head back again and her lips meet mine. Her hands slide out of my hair and she's holding my face like she owns me. A tiny moan escapes her lips as she kisses me hard and then again softly, her hips rocking in my hands. I'm about to pick her up and try to walk us down the hall without running into anything when she ends the kiss and sighs, kissing me softly one more time.

"Final clinical round today," she kisses me again. "I have to go." She kisses me again, slowly. When she breaks the kiss, I tighten my arms a tiny bit. Kissing along the side of her neck, I let my beard tickle her, kissing her lips one more time before letting her go, my hands sliding down her thighs.

"Stupid last day," she mutters under her breath, and I smile as she shifts to stand in front of me, one hand on my chest.

"I love it when you smile," she says softly, her fingers trailing through my beard. Taking her hand, I kiss her fingers.

"I'll be here when you get back."

This is a Job for Pepper Spray

❧

Wren

I could kiss that cat for tripping my dumb ass straight into Kane's lap. Here I was, being so damn careful not to mention last night and our little encounter...If I believed in fate, I would say I just got a very un-subtle nudge and it feels pretty damn right. I did NOT want to walk out that door. Kane's lips and the tickle of his beard and his hands holding my hips and his arms wrapping around my waist and *ohmygod*. I think he's potentially interested in being more than friends...

Laughing to myself, I walk into the hospital. It's an easy shift, I'm paired up with Jenna again, and the doctor spends some time talking about our upcoming matches rather than rapid fire clinical questions today. Grabbing a quick lunch with Jenna, she looks at me closely.

"What?" I smile at her, feeling self conscious.

"Did you get laid?" She asks bluntly, a smile stretching her lips.

"No! What the hell?" I'm completely flustered and I can feel my cheeks heating up.

"Hmm, too bad, the beard burn on your neck suggests some action. I thought maybe you were finally taking advantage of tall, hot and muscl-y," Jenna laughs even harder when I adjust my collar, laughing begrudgingly.

"A little action, yes...I just don't know if it's a good time to start anything, but, with Kane, I don't even care, you know? He just seems worth it...we could figure it out..." I trail off embarrassed. Jenna nods sagely, steepling her fingers in front of her and pursing her lips.

"Diagnosis...L-U-V," she says seriously before cracking a grin.

* * *

Finishing out the shift, we walk to our cars together. Sketching a wave at Jenna, I get in my car, feeling a fluttery set of nerves building in my gut as I drive home. Do Kane and I need to talk about what all this means? Can we just see where it goes? Am I overthinking this, and can I just walk in the apartment and pick back up where we left off? *Yes, let's go with option C.*

Weirdly, the door is unlocked when I arrive. Letting myself in, I smell food. Did he order us dinner? What the-...there are lit candles on the tiny kitchen table. Dinner for two is laid out neatly. *This doesn't feel right. Unless he had help or his vision improved drastically...*

"There you are Wrenny-penny! I've been waiting *ages* for

you to get back!" Bradley comes walking up the short hall from my bedroom. *Where the fuck is Kane?*

"What are you doing here? Where's Kane?" I demand after a stunned little moment.

"Who, that big thug that said he was a friend of yours from Georgia?" Bradley scoffs and rolls his eyes, "I sent him away, called him a cab and told him you don't have time to be playing nurse-maid when you should be celebrating the end of clinicals." He curls his lip in derision as he continues, "Some *friend*, Wren. I can assure you we'll find more suitable *girl*friends for you to associate with this summer."

Waving his hand at me as if everything he has just said is sane and normal, Bradley tries to herd me to a chair. Holding my bag tight to my side, I refuse to move.

"Get the fuck out of my apartment, this has crossed so many lines I don't know where to start." *I need to find Kane.*

"I beg your pardon?" Bradley's eyes narrow, the tiniest wrinkle appearing between them.

"I said, get the FUCK out of my apartment." Bradley takes a couple of steps closer to me and I step to the side, behind a chair, giving him a clear line to the door without coming any closer to me.

"You little bitch. Do you *know* who I am?" His mouth twists with anger, the words spitting out.

"A jackass all day?" I'm pissed now, I never asked for this, never even encouraged him after we went on a couple of dates and there was really nothing there. Reaching in my bag, my hand closes comfortingly around a small can of pepper spray. Stepping further to the side, I jerk my head at the door.

"Get out. Now."

"Solve the problem, Wren. Don't panic, panic makes you stupid."

I can hear my Gran as if she were in the room.

He takes several steps straight at me and I don't know if he's planning to yell at me or try to grab me but he's too close and I pull out the pepper spray. He doesn't slow down and when his hand closes on my wrist I give him a face full. He screams and I take advantage of the opportunity to swing the door open, shove him out in the hall, and slam my door shut behind him, flipping the deadbolt. Grabbing my phone, I call 911. *This is kind of getting to be a habit.* I'm breathing hard, but calm. *Problem solved for now Gran.*

Bradley is still sobbing and wiping his eyes on his coat in the hallway when the police arrive. He's too pissed to lie, just calls me a stupid bitch a few times and they stuff him in the squad car. My apartment reeks of pepper spray, so I get Max in his pet carrier, pack his stuff into my car, open all the windows, and head down the hall to pack a bag for a couple of days.

When I walk in my room, my stomach turns. Bradley lit candles and arranged rose petals in a huge heart on the bed. I have no idea where he got the idea I was interested enough to continue dating, much less *sleep* with him. *I hope his match is in rural North Dakota...or Alaska...or the moon...anything far away from me.*

Letting out a frustrated little scream of disgust, I blow out the candles, open the window and the screen. Grabbing the corners of the comforter, I pick it up with all the roses inside and hold the damn thing out the window, letting the petals float to the lawn below. Dragging it back in, I shut the screen but leave the window open, because it smells like he *sprayed* something in here too.

I swear on my Gran, if that idiot sprayed some kind of deer-piss pheromone-shit in my bed, I will go find him tomorrow and pepper spray his stupid face again.

Stomping back out to the kitchen, I throw all the food away, *he probably roofied mine, the slimeball,* and blow out the candles.

I'm sure Bradley won't be at the police station for more than five minutes, his dad is some important businessman in town. Honestly, I just hope he learned his lesson and there's no blowback. At least he told the cops everything, and I can't worry about that right now anyway. I've got to find Kane, and then I've probably got to stay in a hotel at least one night. Texting Jenna, I tell her what happened with Bradley, and she calls me immediately.

"Ohmygod Wren, are you okay? Where was Kane?" Her voice is full of anger and concern.

"I don't know where Kane went, Bradley gave him some story about us still being together." The list of places he would go without being able to see is, hopefully, short.

"You can stay with me until your apartment clears," Jenna announces. "And I'm going to call my Dad and make sure he tells Bradley's dad what that assface did when they golf next Tuesday. What else can I do to help?" She's so nice. *I'm regretting all the times I called her a bitch in my head for being perfect.*

"Thanks, you're awesome…is it too much to ask you to watch Max? I've got to find Kane and I'd rather Max didn't revenge pee in my car." *Please don't hate cats, please don't hate cats.*

"…Is Max a…child?" After a pause, Jenna's question strikes me as hilarious. I'm sure it's an adrenaline rush from the last hour slamming into me, but I can barely stop laughing long enough to answer.

"No, he's my cat." I stutter out the words in between laughing. Jenna lets out an exaggerated sigh of relief and laughs with me.

"Oh thank god, I love cats. Kids? Not my thing."

Not Into Engaged Chicks

*K*ane

"I'll have another, Joe." It won't help, but a couple of beers will make me sleep hard and that's mostly the goal at this point.

Engaged. Why didn't she tell me? Some guy who sounds all polished with money showed up, *Bradley.*

"Why would Wren complete an act this charitable at one of the busiest and most important junctures of her life?" Bradley sneered when he found out she was helping me. *Good question, Bradley.* I wasn't sure what to think until he brought up the girl's night she was on that night at Joe's. It hadn't even occurred to me that it was a hen party for *her.*

So she went slumming…with me…I wonder how she thought that was going to go…a quick fling before she settled down to be 'Mrs. Bradley'? I managed to voice command a cab on my phone and headed for Joe's. He'll drive me back to my place when he closes up.

"This won't help you know," Joe's gravelly voice is worried as he sets another beer in my hand.

"Won't help what?" I'm not in the mood to talk and I don't want pity.

"You, to forget. Don't bullshit me and say nothing is going on either, I've been running this bar for 35 years, son." I hear glasses clinking as Joe moves around behind the bar. The vision in my right eye is better today, I can even see some color, but everything is still blurry.

"Fair enough. I don't want to forget her. I just want to sleep." It hurts. Wren's not who I thought she was, and I'm not in the mood to feel anything. The bell over the door jingles, I usually wouldn't be able to hear it, but it's early and the bar is pretty empty.

"What can I get ya?" Joe asks the newcomer.

"I'll have what he's having," Wren says, settling onto the stool beside me.

"What are you doing here, Wren?" This wasn't how I pictured my night ending when she left this morning.

"I came to find you, obviously, I was worried when you were gone." She sounds confused. "What did Bradley tell you?"

"He told me enough, there's not much to talk about if you're going to be a married woman." Engaged, *to that jackass.*

"Marr-, that son of a-...yeah, I *can't even* with that asshole right now." Wren keeps muttering, apparently so annoyed she can't speak, and I hear her fingernails clicking out an irritated staccato on the bar. After a moment, she sucks in a breath, blowing it out hard.

"He's in jail, likely still crying over the pepper spray I doused him with, by the way." She sounds a lot pissed and a little amused, and…

"You…pepper spray?"

"Uh, *yeah*, that's what you do to idiots that show up at your house, kick out your guest, and act like a candle light dinner for two and rose petals on the bed is *super normal* for people who *aren't even dating*." Her voice is full of sarcasm.

"Not dating?" *I need to stop, I sound like a fucking parrot.* Wren scoffs and bumps her shoulder into mine.

"No, most *definitely* not dating…we went out on three-and-a-half dates, and that was three too many, he's a spoiled mama's boy, and a serious control-freak."

"I was stupid to listen to him. I should have been there to keep you safe." *I can't believe I took that idiot's word for everything. I was so sure having a chance with Wren wasn't in the cards for me.* My heart stutters just thinking about her getting hurt.

"My Gran taught me not to wait for anyone else to take care of my problems," her voice is soft. "I just might give you my heart though, I'll need you to keep that safe for me." I hear her swallow and then a clink as Wren sets the bottle on the bar and gets off her stool.

"I promise," I whisper, and then I just listen, waiting. Glancing over my shoulder, I can make out that she's crossing the room.

Music fills the bar as she picks songs on the old jukebox in the corner. She plays our song first. Crossing the room she lays a hand on my arm. I cover it with my own.

"You remembered." *It might weird her out if I call it our song.*

"Of course, it's *our* song after all," I can hear that she's smiling and my heart thumps hard. "Dance with me, Kane."

Standing, I let her lead me out to the little tile dance floor. The song is slow and *this* time I pull her in close. One of her arms goes around my waist and I hold her other hand tucked into my heart. I rest my cheek in her hair, and I'm home.

We dance all night, not really caring if the music is fast or slow, I'm not letting go of her again. When Joe makes last call, she links her fingers through mine and leads me to her car.

"Wren?"

"Yeah?"

"Before we go anywhere else can we stop and get my truck?" A laugh bursts out of her, and I'm sure she's looking at me folded up like a pretzel in the passenger side of her little car.

"Absolutely."

Just Us

Wren

Kane's door is ajar when we pull up behind the building and climb the stairs to his apartment. I gasp when I notice, and he immediately tucks me behind him.

"What's wrong?" He keeps his voice quiet. He's obviously remembering the guys I saw the other day too.

"The door is open a few inches." I whisper, leaning around him to try and see if there are any lights on inside. We stand quietly for a moment, and I look down the alley, from our vantage point at the top of the stairs I can't see any cars but my own and Kane's truck.

"There's no other cars, I think whoever was here is gone." I whisper, staying behind him. Swiping my phone open, I turn on the flashlight.

"Shove the door open?" I'm nervous, so my whisper is barely a squeak as I point my phone light at the doorway. Kane nods and reaches out in front of him, pausing when his fingers reach the door and then giving it a push. We both listen for a moment, and then I reach past him and flip on the light in the hall. *We should probably call the cops, this is stupid.*

"I don't see anything, but it looks like something is broken on the floor of the kitchen." I can see bits of glass shining in the dim light of the hall, "So they probably looked around for whatever it was that they wanted. I bet they're gone." I wonder if he's ready to share...he obviously knows more about all this than he's letting on.

"Do you know who they are, or what they want Kane?" At my words, his head drops a little and he sighs.

"Yeah." He sounds unhappy, and shoulders his way through the door.

"Oh, geez, okay," I scurry in after him, reaching for light switches as we go. When we reach the kitchen, I start describing the damage.

"All the cupboards are open, it looks like a jar or glass got broken on the floor, but that's about it." I take him around the biggest pieces of glass to the living room.

"Um...it looks like they just pulled sofa cushions and emptied your bookshelf." *I wonder if they had to bail quickly because the police showed up, I hope so.* I stuff the cushions back on the sofa, and close the books that landed open on the floor. I'm relieved to see the plant, safe on the little table.

"I bet your 911 call spooked them off, or else they had to come back later and be quick." He grumbles, walking forward carefully. He reaches in the bedroom door and turns on the light. I get up from where I'm piling books and walk into the bedroom.

"It's pretty much the same in here. Dresser drawers are open, clothes all over the floor, bed messed up." Kane nods, turning back to the living room, he walks to the sofa, and sits down.

"Come here," he rumbles, holding out his hand. A rush of heat zings me straight in the hoo-ha at his words, and I walk over, putting my hand in his. He pulls me in close, his hands sliding around my waist to rest on my butt. He hugs me in tight, his head on my chest. I twine my fingers in his hair, and we just stay that way a moment.

My brain chooses to chime in at this point and I have a mini-argument with myself.

Brain: You've known him for less than a week.

Heart: Fuck off, I've known him for four years.

Brain: You know nothing about him.

Heart: I know he's important to me, and I know I really like the way he just put his hands on my butt.

Brain: That is not logical, and he's got baggage.

Heart: Fuck logic, and who doesn't have baggage?

Brain: Very mature.

Heart: We. Have. A. Song.

Brain: *Sigh*...fine...well played Heart.

Heart: Thank you.

Unaware of my internal battle, Kane tilts his head back, eyes closed, silently asking to be kissed, and I comply. *Heart cheers, brain sulks and then shrugs and gets on board with this plan.*

At first he lets me lay little kisses across the seam of his lips, and then I feel one of his hands slide up my back and tangle in my hair. His lips part, he pulls me in tighter and Kane *kisses* me.

Kane kisses me so hard I see stars and my knees get weak. I

close my eyes tight and kiss him back and wish I didn't have to breathe, because I never want to stop. This crazy day and all the things he hasn't told me yet just fade away. I let myself lean into him and he turns us, laying me down on the couch beside him without breaking the kiss.

I feel the muscles of his back roll as he holds his weight up off me, and his hips shift, pushing between my knees. I have to break the kiss with a strangled gasp as he surges forward, and I can't stop the automatic rocking of my hips, trying to bring him closer, my head thrown back as I lose myself in how good it feels to have him this close.

He kisses down my neck with a groan, his hand sliding under my shirt. Reaching down, I pull up on the back of his shirt, wanting to feel his skin, cursing the jeans we're both wearing. He pushes up with one hand and reaches back with the other, pulling his shirt off in one smooth motion.

"That is so fucking hot," I whisper, and he smiles, rocking his hips forward again, his hand sliding back under my shirt to play along the lace of my bra. He leans down, finding my neck with his lips and gently bites and kisses his way back to my mouth. My hips have completely taken on a life of their own, my hands are trailing down his ribs and exploring the muscles of his back, and we're moving together. His lips consume me, the urgency and heat and desire in his kisses burning a trail straight to my heart. I can't think, I don't want to breathe, I just want this moment.

Sorry to Break Up the Party

*K*ane

I can't think straight. The smell of Wren's hair, the softness of her skin, the way she sighs…the heat of her as we move together, her hips rocking, pulling me closer. The way she kisses me back like she's branding me.

"Mmmm Kane," she sighs, fingers trailing down my ribs to the button of my jeans. "Do you want to go to the bedroom?" Her voice is soft and perfect and she is magic. Lifting my head from that sweet spot at the side of her neck, I look down at her. Really look. She's blonde and I can see her big eyes, and her smile, but it's as if we're underwater. I can't see enough, not yet.

"Yes I do." I kiss her lips softly, "I've wanted you in my arms since the second you walked out of that little yellow house in Gravity." I kiss her again. "I wanted you when you showed up at that bar in the middle of nowhere." Another kiss. "Baby,

I want to take you to bed more than I want to breathe." She wiggles her hips as I kiss her again.

"But…" she whispers.

"But when I feel you clench around me for the first time, I want to be able to *see* you when you scream my name," I growl in her ear.

"Ohmygod," she gasps and moves her hips again, and all my willpower is almost out the window. She's kissing me, holding the sides of my face as she sucks in my lip and lets me feel her teeth. Sliding a hand behind her back, I lift her up as I sit up on the couch, and she ends up straddling me, her hair falling around both of us.

"Fuck you're amazing," she whispers dragging her nails lightly down my chest. A buzzing from the couch beside us makes her jump. My phone must have fallen out of my pants, and as I reach to silence it, Wren bursts into giggles.

"Kane?" She snickers, "I'm sorry, but, 'Dad-Ass Motherfucker' is calling you." *Fuck.*

"I'll call him later," reaching for the phone, I swipe down and toss it face down on the coffee table. Just as her fingers start to trail up my arm, it starts vibrating again. *Fucker, not now, don't you fucking dare ruin this moment.*

"Maybe he needs to talk to you now?" Wren whispers playfully. "And I think I need the back story on his contact name." She giggles again, giving me a little pinch on the arm. Reaching behind her, she hands me the phone as it goes silent.

"See, it's fine I'll call him la-", fucking phone starts buzzing again.

"He put that contact name in himself," I grump, holding the still buzzing phone. "My old man got drunk and figured out how to save numbers on the same day, I don't know why I didn't change it." *It's kind of sad really, but he was so damn proud of how clever he was, and he showed it to me like a kid bringing home an 'A' paper from school.*

The phone has been silent for a moment. It starts buzzing again. I swipe it open and answer the call this time.

"Yeah."

Wren gives my beard a little tug and climbs off my lap, wandering out to the kitchen. I hear her closing cabinet doors. She must have gone in the laundry next, because that's where I had a broom, and I hear her sweeping up the glass, humming to herself.

"Kane, please don't hang up, it's Crystal." Hearing her sad little baby-doll voice, I sigh, already sorry I answered.

"What'd he do this time?" I ask, but I don't even care.

"He didn't come home last night," …*that's it?*

"I know, that's nothing new," Crystal whimpers, "but I had a bad feeling, you know how I get those feelings Kane. So I read my cards and The Ten of Swords wouldn't stop coming up and I thought I was gonna barf." Crystal starts talking faster and faster, wanting to get the story out.

"So I called the hospitals and he wasn't in any of them, but then…" she starts crying in earnest and I have to wait a minute while she calms down enough to keep talking.

"But then…his buddy Johnny calls me up and asks where he is, and I say I haven't seen him since last night. He gets me all worried because he said he left him sitting on a bar stool at Mick's." She squeaks out the last few words and starts crying harder.

"Crystal stop crying, what *happened*?" I look towards the kitchen and see Wren turn to look at me. Dumping the glass from the dustpan she's holding into the trash, she sets the broom in the corner and comes back to the couch.

"So I get in my car and head over to Mick's to see if he knows anything and there's an ambulance in the alley behind." Crystal breaks down again. I'm gripping the phone hard at this point, willing her to tell me *what the fuck happened*, but I know if I tell her to pull herself together she'll never finish the story.

"I need you to tell me what happened," I speak as calmly as I am able, and Crystal quiets as Wren curls up beside me on the couch. I wait for Crystal to continue.

"He died, Kane. They found him in the alley. They found him by the stairs coming out of the bar and it looked like he fell and hit his head…there was blood in his hair," Crystal says softly, and then there's silence on the line, broken only by Crystal crying.

"Kane? Are you still there?" Crystal asks after a long moment, and then she gives a little hiccup.

"I'm here." It seems so surreal, I wait for the other shoe to drop, for her to put my old man on the phone so he can yell a drunken, 'got ya dumbass!' I hear Crystal blow her nose, hard.

"I don't know what to do, Kane." *Every part of me wants to tell her this is not my problem and hang up.*

"Text me your address. I'll come out and take care of things." I can't make my voice sound any nicer. I don't want to do this, I don't want to believe he's gone. My old man had nine fucking lives, only to wind up dead in an alley. *And no one killed him... define irony.*

"Okay, thanks Kane." Crystal whispers. "I'm sorry."

"Yeah, me too Crystal." I disconnect and sit there a minute, stunned.

"It doesn't sound like everything is okay," Wren says hesitantly, her hand lightly drawing a comforting pattern on my thigh.

"No, it's not…" I sigh, lifting my arm up over her head and tucking her into my side. "My father died." She gasps, her hand reaching up for my face.

"Oh, Kane! Ohmygod, was there an accident or something?"

"Yeah…he fell and hit his head on some cement stairs. That's what they think happened right now." It doesn't even feel real when I say it out loud. "I've got to go to Vegas and take care of things."

"I'm coming with you." Wren says firmly. I don't even want to argue. I can't see well enough to go alone, and I want her to come. I need to tell her everything. She sucks in a little breath.

"What else can I do to help? This is just…I don't even know what to say…I'm so sorry Kane." She whispers with a little quiver in her voice.

"Don't cry for him Wren. He doesn't deserve that from you." I sound harsh, but not one tear for him, not after everything.

"I'm sorry…you weren't very close then?" Wren whispers.

"Don't be sorry," I hug her tighter, "I shouldn't take it out on you, I'm sorry about that, but no, we weren't…this is just one last job I have to do."

"Okay…" Wren pauses, "If that's the case, do you think… you could wait a day? I hate to ask, but the doctor wants to see you tomorrow morning to take the mesh off your eye." She sounds hesitant to even bring it up.

"Yeah, I'm not going to make you miss Match Day either. It sounds like a big deal." At my words she snorts lightly.

"It's pretty huge, but they'll send me regardless, I can miss it."

"I go to the doctor, you go to your ceremony. I bet they won't release him for a couple days anyway." I'm not making her change one single thing, she's worked too hard.

99

"Do you think you'd like to come?" She asks quietly. "It's okay if you don't, if you want to just sleep or think or make phone calls or I don't kn-" I cut her off.

"I wouldn't miss it." She pulls my head down and kisses me, and this time it's different. She's here, she's with me, we'll get through this and then maybe we'll have time to see where this leads. Right now, her kiss is full of comfort and promise. I stand up, take her hand, and lead her into the bedroom.

"I want to hold you," I whisper, hoping she'll hear what I can't say yet.

"I want to hold you too," she whispers shyly.

I Won't Bite...Hard

W*ren*

Waking up in Kane's arms is exactly as wonderful as I expected it to be. He's snoring softly, one arm pillowing my head, the other loosely slung over my hips as he spoons me. Asleep or not, he's also happy that I'm here, and the evidence is pressed against my ass. *A LOT of evidence, oh my...* My heart starts doing roll-call to get my lady bits in action, and I would *realllly* like to wake him up and jump his bones right now.

"When I feel you clench around me for the first time, I want to be able to see you when you scream my name." Kane's words whisper through my head in that perfect growl, and I shiver. Those words, so full of deliciously dirty promise make me behave. It's only fair, he wants to make, and watch...me scream his name... *my clit just about literally exploded with joy.*

Letting my eyes drift shut, I doze, and daydream a little, not wanting to leave his warmth or the weight of his arm. Finally, my bladder forces me out of bed. Kane shifts and rolls onto his back, but he doesn't wake up. I stop and admire the view, his face is softer when he's sleeping, the worry line between his brows is smooth, lips relaxed and begging to be kissed. The muscles of his abs tense and my breath comes a little faster as he rolls back onto his side. When his hand hits the spot where I was, he stirs. I turn and quick-walk to the bathroom because:

I was watching him sleep like a creepy stalker.

I still really need to pee.

I linger in the bathroom a minute, and then realize that's a bad idea for a few reasons, *this is the only bathroom and he might think I'm pooping top the list.* Checking my hair quick, *yep flat on one side, bird nest on the other, awesome,* I walk back into the bedroom.

Kane is sitting on the edge of the bed, he's pulled on sweatpants and a t-shirt, and he looks my direction.

"I can see clearer today," he says with a grin, and my heart melts because I've been so damn worried the damage was irreversible. Walking over, I take his face in my hands, looking at the stitches that still need to be removed. He's got both eyes open, looking up at me and I can see the mesh on his left eye, fogging his vision.

"Hopefully that little thing has done its job," while I've got his face right there, I kiss him. *It's kind of all I want to do lately...* His hands fit around my waist like a belt, and he stands, lifting me right up with him, lips still smashed against mine. I wrap my legs around his waist and feel him, hard and ready, underneath me. I'm only wearing underwear and one of his t-shirts and his thumbs brush across my nipples as he walks forward, pressing my back into the wall, his hips rocking into me.

Kane's sweatpants and the thin lace of my underwear don't stop me from feeling the heat. He's grinding against the perfect spot, and I am *so* turned on. My arms around his neck, I hold tight and press my face against his collar bone, finding that sensitive spot, sucking in and biting it gently. Maybe not as gentle as I thought, because Kane jerks and groans and then his hips press harder, rocking faster right over my center. He bows his head and leaves a line of kisses along the curve of my breast, marking me with each one. His hips move even faster, pushing against me harder, and clothes or not, I can feel the spiral building. I let my head fall back against the wall. *Jesustakethewheel he can make me come without taking my clothes off...*

I want him to rip my underwear off, I want the layers gone, I want him to drive into me, pounding me against the wall. As I'm riding that fine line, Kane kisses his way up my neck and his hips keep rocking. I can't wait another second to fall off that delicious cliff, and Kane lifts his head, his face intense.

"Come for me, Baby,"

As the words roll from his lips...I do.

Heart Eyes

Kane

"Considering your condition the night this happened Mr. Morgan," the doctor's cool voice is quiet as she carefully removes the stitches from my forehead, "you are extremely lucky to have such a good result already." I feel another little tug, and then I hear a clink as she sets her tools down on a tray beside me.

"I'm going to take the antibiotic mesh out now, and then I'll need to flush the area." The lights dim, and I hear the nurse move closer. She holds a cloth or gauze or something to the side of my face.It doesn't take long and the mesh is out, my eye has been flooded with drops and saline and I don't know what else.

"All finished," the doctor says crisply, moving away as the nurse finishes wiping away the drops that found their way down the side of my face.

"I'm going to give Donovan a couple of new scripts, one is for a final round of antibiotics, the other is for drops that you can use as often as you need to for dry eye." The doctor chuckles, "And we'll give you one more pair of these amazing sunglasses, I understand you've had a hard time keeping track of them." The nurse laughs quietly too, they both know I'm going to throw the damn things away again.

"Thanks Doc...am I going to get full vision back in the left eye? My right eye is getting better all the time, I'm able to see details unless I'm tired."

"Well, the impact of the bottle damaged your iris, so along with the cuts to your cornea, your pupil has changed shape slightly. That may cause some blurring or color blindness, it's too soon to tell." I can hear her fingernails tapping on the keyboard of the computer at the counter.

"My pupil is not a circle?" *The hell? How does that work?*

"Not a perfect circle, no, it's a little more of an organic shape now, but it's not your dominant eye, and we just have to wait and see what you get back." Standing, the doctor waits for me to stand up too.

"I'll see you in two weeks, Mr. Morgan, and then we can stretch it to a month or so if everything continues to improve." The doctor leaves the room, and the nurse leads me out to the waiting room. *At least I can see well enough not to hold onto her shoulder this time.* I hate needing help.

Wren is chatting with a different nurse, and my heart squeezes when she turns to me and smiles.

"All set?" She takes a couple papers from the nurse, "Thanks Cindy, see you later."

"Sure thing, Wren, take care." Nurse Cindy gives me a complete once-over, eyes gleaming with curiosity. I pretend not to notice.

"I called Jenna, she's good with Max until we get back from Vegas," Wren smiles, "he's got his claws in deep, she was sweet-talking him while she's on the phone with me, I think she's trying to rename him Pookie."

"That's good, I wasn't sure you'd still want to go, I can see pretty good now, well enough to get around." I glance at her carefully. I don't want to give her an out, I want her to go, but it only seems fair.

"So you don't want me to come with you?" Her eyes are confused and a little hurt.

"Yes, I do, I just…want you to come because…you want to be…with me…" I trail off, I don't know how to say what I want to without sounding like an idiot. *It might already be too late.* It feels like losing my eyes for a short time has made me lose everything I used to rely on, and I'm floundering around like a newborn colt.

I grew up with a man who sneered at weakness and beat it down every chance he got. Feelings? *Stomp them.* Emotional responses? *Stomp them.* I'm not equipped to deal with all of the things I'm feeling for Wren. All the strength and power I've got and I'm weak. It makes me angry at myself.

"Okay, so…to set the record straight," Wren says firmly, "I wouldn't go to Vegas unless I was 'in' with you, like, let's-see-where-this-is-going-hope-it's-a-long-way, 'in'." We get to my truck and climb in, but she doesn't turn the key. She looks at me seriously, a blush coloring her cheeks.

"I don't know why it feels right to jump in with both feet with you." Wren shakes her head, "I'm probably saying too much now, but *you* feel right to me. You felt right the night we met, and then you were gone, and I had to put that little

106

broken piece away because I didn't know how to handle it. I mean, what was I supposed to do? You left. And then we meet again at that bar, and it was like lightning striking twice, and I just don't want to waste anymore time. Kane, you *feel* right." Wren sighs. "I'm sorry…I probably sound like an idiot, it's just weird, I want you to get it." She sighs again, "I'm rambl-"

"I do get it," I whisper, cutting her off, as I reach over and scoop her up and pull her into my lap right there in the truck. I don't want to mess this up by trying to talk anymore. Wren turns on my lap and straddles me as I slide my hands under her shirt. She gasps and bends her head, claiming my mouth, demanding, hot. *Thank fuck she got a terrible spot in the back forty of this parking lot.* When we finally break apart, breath coming fast, she looks into my eyes. Really looks, for the first time since they took the mesh out.

"Kane, your eye…" Wren murmurs, and my brows draw together as she looks at me, I didn't look at my 'organic' pupil yet.

"Yeah," I frown, "the doctor said my pupil isn't round anymore…does it look bad? I didn't look yet."

"It's shaped like a heart now," she breathes, "your beautiful eyes, so perfect."

"A heart?"

She nods, a smile stretching her lips, *if she likes it, I like it.* I reach up and pull her head back down to mine, kissing her so thoroughly she lets out a giggle when we part again.

Time To Spill the Beans

W^{ren}

Jenna gives me a discreet little wave from further down the row as we file into Match Day in alphabetical order. I wave back, and then scan the audience, looking for Kane. He's not hard to pick out and I try not to blush when I look at him, because *damn*. Black cashmere sweater, pushed up to the elbows, a dark grey t-shirt peeking out at the collar, dark jeans, and black boots. He's a bad-boy wet dream, sitting in an auditorium...*for me.*

An hour and a half later, I meet him outside the auditorium for the reception. Jenna is by my side, bubbling because she got her first choice, and I'm laughing, caught up in her excitement. I'm excited too, I'm going home to Georgia.

Kane's face seems a little tense, but he smiles when I walk up to him and pulls me into a one-armed hug, so I don't ask if everything is okay. Jenna immediately starts peppering him with questions, but he quickly turns the tables on her by bringing up Max. Out comes her phone with pictures and videos, and I'm starting to worry that my cat has been adopted.

"Don't worry Wren, I'll give him back," Jenna drawls, reading my mind. She makes a face, "Anyway, I've heard cats vomit if you put them in the car after they're past the kitten stage, and I don't know if the trip to Pennsylvania would work out at all."

"That might make the trip to Georgia interesting, but I'll risk it," I counter, laughing, "I'll pick him up in a few days when we get back from Las Vegas."

"Of course, and Kane, I'm so sorry to hear about your father," Jenna says sincerely, her hand on his arm.

"Thanks." Kane's voice is gruff, but he gives her a nod.

"And speaking of," I glance at Kane, "we actually need to head for the airport, soon, so we're going to bail."

"Okay cave-girl, call me when you get back," Jenna squeezes my arm and gives Kane a wink, heading off to mingle.

"Cave-girl?" Kane sounds amused, and I look up to see him grinning at me.

"Ha, yeah, she thinks it's funny after that night at Joe's when those guys were bothering us."

"I've been meaning to ask you where you learned your moves," Kane says, letting go of my waist, he takes my hand and we head for the door.

"Oh, um, well, my Gran doesn't believe in damsels in distress. She told me I needed to know enough to slow them down until I could get away or get an audience." It feels weird talking about this with him, he's huge, he wouldn't have to use tricks like what Gran taught me.

"She sounds like a smart lady, why an audience?" he asks as we get into his truck.

"She said bullies back down when there are witnesses, it just makes sense I guess."

"There were a lot of people in that bar when he tried to dance with your friend though," Kane counters.

"Yes, but after I thumped him and called his buddies out, they backed off real quick. He was just too stupid." I shrug, "It's not an exact science or anything." Kane laughs.

"That's true enough. If I had my way you'd never need to take care of an idiot like that again, but I'm glad you can." His words make me blush, I was worried that he would think I was silly for standing up to people bigger than me. *I've dated more than one guy that felt threatened because I don't play the 'hand fluttering princess' role well.*

We stop at my apartment to shut all the windows. The pepper spray has dissipated, and I pack a new bag for the trip. Locking up, we head for the airport, Kane's got a bag in the truck he packed earlier this morning. It's about an hour drive, seems like as good a time as any to see if Kane will open up a little.

"What brought you to Gravity in the first place?" I ask quietly, glancing at him before looking back at the road. It's a beautiful clear day, the sun is shining, not much traffic. I relax, content to drive and wait.

"I was running away," Kane mutters quietly, "from pretty much everything, but mostly from my old man and all the problems he kept making mine." He stares out the window a minute before he continues.

"Yeah, if we're gonna make a go of this, you need to know everything," Kane sighs heavily, "I just hope you want to stick around after I tell you."

Her Third Eye is Drunk

Kane

I tell Wren a little about growing up with a fighter. About my mom dying, and how things changed. Getting into fighting, and getting back out of fighting. I tell her about having to fix fights.

I don't sugar coat what I did to get my dad out of trouble, I was a heavy collecting money for a thug. I tell her that on the day I paid off the debt, my old man got stupid and stole a wad of cash and a ring from our boss.

I tell her that Smitty is probably motivated enough to keep looking, and my dad being dead probably won't change his need for revenge.

"Best guess, those guys that you saw at my place heard my name over a police scanner or a little mention about the arrest, they keep an eye on those," I explain tipping back my beer for a final swallow and signalling the bartender.

My storytelling took us all the way to the airport. We've checked in and we're sitting at a bar near our gate. I've never said so many words strung together, in a row, in my entire life. Wren is listening intently, she stops me once in a while to ask questions, otherwise she's just absorbing the story. *I can't tell what she thinks, her face is serious, but not upset or disgusted at the shit-show that has been my life.*

"You never know, Kane, if this guy hears your dad is gone, he may decide enough is enough." Wren looks hopeful, her hand in mine.

"I hope so, there's no way to tell really. If he hears I'm back in Georgia I can expect a visit." I admit quietly. I don't want her to worry, but I know Smitty's got operations close enough to Gravity that word might get back to him.

"So you'll come back to Georgia with me?" Wren says softly, eyes shining.

"There's nothing for me in Texas." It's true, I was just biding time. "I can work anywhere."

"Let's take care of business and then we can go home, Kane." Wren winks. "Come what may."

It's not worth talking about, and I don't want her to worry, so what I don't tell Wren is if Smitty or his guys call me, I'll leave her behind. *That* business is mine to take care of, alone. When they call boarding for our flight, Wren loops her arm through mine, she seems content with what I've told her for now. Before we even start taxiing for takeoff, she's sleeping on my shoulder.

Landing in Las Vegas, I hail us a cab and give the driver Crystal's address. We arrive at a neighborhood just a block off the Strip, and I have no idea how my old man could swing living here until I see their place. The address is a tiny little house, squeezed between a convenience store and a motel. There's a beat up fence, and a sidewalk about ten feet long leads to three broken front steps. I can see a light on through one of the windows.

"Oh Kane! Sweetie it's so good to see you, I don't know what to do with *anything!*" Crystal answers when I knock, and it's pretty immediately clear that she's drunk. It's five in the afternoon, she's either already in pajamas or didn't bother to get dressed for the day, and her makeup is badly smudged under her eyes. Throwing herself in my arms with a wail, she starts sobbing, and I have to half carry her back into the house.

Crystal's shoulders shake under her thin robe and she tries to light a cigarette, but her hands are shaking so badly she can't work the lighter. I reach over and take it, holding it while she gets a light.

"Thank you Sweetie, you always were one of the good ones," Crystal says in her baby-doll voice, with a brilliant smile that just looks wrong with her greasy hair and smeared eyeliner. Taking a couple of long drags, she looks me over and then turns her bloodshot eyes to Wren.

"I didn't know Kane had a woman," she lets out an annoyed huff. I can tell Wren isn't sure what to say, but she looks offended and she opens her mouth to respond, so I jump in first.

"It's not like we were in touch, Crystal, simmer down. The only time we spoke was when you needed something." I snort at her, sitting heavily on the couch opposite her as Wren comes closer and perches on the arm. I loop an arm around her hips and she smiles, putting a hand on my shoulder.

"Well obviously if you'd been around more, he'd probably still be here," Crystal sneered. "He only got to drinking bad when you left." It's a drunken jab and I don't take the bait.

"Sober up Crystal. I'm sorry you're hurting. We'll come back tomorrow and get all of his stuff." I stand back up abruptly. I'm not starting into this with her and she's Jonesing for a fight. It won't work, and it won't make her feel better. I know she's missing that asshole.

"The fuck you will," Crystal slurs swaying as she scowls at me. "I'll light all that shit on fire in the yard if you don't take it now. It's the boxes in the bedroom. Get it and get the fuck out of my house." She stumbles through an archway leading to the kitchen and slams the fridge door open against the wall. I hear the clink as she opens a bottle and she comes out with a red plastic cup full to the brim. *I should not have had Wren come here, I know better than this, she should have stayed at the hotel.*

"Bo-xes?" Crystal contemptuously waves a hand in the direction of a door off to the left, taking a large gulp of her drink, spilling some in the process. She refuses to look at me as I stand up, and Wren is close behind. Stepping into the bedroom, I look around.

"She seemed a lot nicer on the phone," Wren whispers, and I look back at her.

"She's a lot nicer when she's not a bottle deep," I grumble back. "Sorry you had to see her like this, I should have had you hang out at the hotel." This is nothing new, I'm just feeling stupid for bringing Wren.

"No, it's okay, I'm glad you aren't alone, I think she'd be worse." Wren's voice is warm and she's probably right. *If Wren wasn't here, Crystal would be trying real hard to get me to fill the spot my old man left, that's for sure.* He always did pick women a lot younger than he was, Crystal is only five years older than I am. It made for a lot of awkward situations once I got into high school.

There's a couple of boxes sitting in the middle of the floor, where Crystal said they'd be, overflowing with clothing and pictures and papers. There's no real rhyme or reason to it, she probably packed them while she was drinking. I quickly glance around the room for things she might have missed, but she's got clothes strewn everywhere.

A couple of picture frames are sticking out of the trash can. Walking over to it, I pull them out carefully. They're pictures of Crystal and my dad, taken a few years ago. She's all dolled up and he's got his hair slicked back, the lights of a casino shining behind them in both pictures as they smile into the camera. The glass is broken in both frames, but I flip open the back of each and take the pictures out. Dropping the broken glass and frames back in the trash, I look around for a place to leave them. She'll want them when she's sober.

"Here, I'll put them in the dresser," Wren says softly, holding out her hand. I reach across the bed and hand them to her. I hear her open the drawer as I walk around the room looking for any sign that my old man lived here for the past few years. *A life pared down to two boxes.*

Shifting the top stuff so it fits better, I fold the boxes closed and stack one on top of the other. Wren silently shuts the drawer and walks ahead of me out to the living room. Crystal is asleep on the sofa. Wren walks over and carefully takes the cup out of her hand, turning and carrying it to the kitchen. Crystal gives a little sigh but doesn't stir.

I set the boxes down and pull out my wallet. Crossing the room, I open the little ceramic cat where she always kept her laundry money and put in five hundred dollars. She'll find it later, it wouldn't do her any good right now anyway. Looking around the room one more time, I watch Wren put a blanket over Crystal and then she straightens, looking at me.

"That was a nice thing to do Kane." She obviously saw me deposit the money in the cat.

"It'll help her get back on her feet, she was with him for a long time, longer than most." I shrug and pick the boxes back up. Wren leads the way out, closing the door softly behind me.

How Are Your Eyes?

ren

W I've got a secret.

I need to share it with Kane, but I don't know how, and I'm not even sure I've got it all figured out. Now isn't the time, not after the tension of Crystal's house, and all the memories that whatever is in those boxes is bound to drum up.

Kane is quieter than usual as we arrive at the hotel. I went ahead and made us reservations at The Mirage on the strip, mostly because I've never been to Las Vegas and I thought, 'why not'. Kane spoke with the police this morning before we flew out and they said it will be another day before they release Kane's father to the crematorium. Two days after that Kane will get his father's ashes.

I don't know what I can do to make this easier for him...he doesn't seem to be grieving. It makes me wonder if he will or if he truly looks at this as one last job, in a long list of shitty jobs, he's had to do involving his father.

"Do you want to go somewhere for dinner? Or would you rather I order us something?" I ask carefully, coming up behind him as he stands at the window, staring down at the lights of the strip. Wrapping my arms around his waist from behind, I rest my cheek on his broad back. One of his hands covers both of mine, and we just stand together for a minute.

"If it's all the same to you, I think maybe I'd like to stay in tonight," his voice rumbles my ear. "I think I'll look through all his shit, see if I need to ship it back or what, I'm sure I won't need to keep everything in those boxes, I might be able to just fit what I want in my bag."

"Of course," I feel like maybe he'll want a little bit of time alone when he opens those boxes, and so I continue. "Actually there was a Chinese place that looked good on the corner and I want to check the gift shop for a little thank you gift for Jenna," I keep my voice light, it feels like all I can do while we're here to help him is to not add any more shadows to his life.

"That sounds good, I can go with you if you want," his voice sounds uncertain, vague, as if he's thinking of other things.

"No, I'll be fine. You take your time with your dad's things." I squeeze him in a hug and before he lets go, he turns and gathers me into his arms.

"I'm glad you're here, Wren." He rumbles. I tilt my face up and he kisses me hard.

"Me too," I gasp, and we both smile when he lets me go. Swinging a jacket around my shoulders to ward off the cooler night air, I grab my wallet and head out into the hallway. The door clicks shut softly behind me.

I take my time browsing through a couple of the shops in the lobby of the hotel and then the ones next to the Chinese place I saw earlier. I find a beautiful little pair of Venetian glass earrings that look like something Jenna would like, and after the saleswoman wraps them up, tuck them into my jacket pocket.

Wandering down to the Chinese restaurant, I take a stool at the walk up bar, order us several entrees and two orders of crab rangoons, and settle in to people-watch while I wait. It doesn't take long, and I hope I've given Kane enough time to look through his father's things without interruption. Returning to the hotel, I find Kane sitting on the edge of the bed facing the window, slowly pulling items out of the first box.

"There's not much here that I want, he wasn't real sentimental," Kane comments gruffly. Shoving the box to the side, he helps me get all the take out boxes out of the bag, and groans with appreciation at the spread of food. We eat in companionable silence, and the long day really starts to kick in as I let out a huge yawn.

"Here we are on the Vegas strip and I made you get takeout and put you to sleep," Kane snorts, shaking his head. "I'm sorry, let's do something tomorrow, get out...explore."

"*You* are *fine*," I stretch, giggling after another yawn makes my jaw crack. "But yes, tomorrow we go exploring, I love this plan." I'm nervous now, because I'd like to shower. I don't know if I'm supposed to awkwardly gather all of my clothes and get fully dressed in the bathroom after our encounter this morning. *And the promise of more...much more. And now I realllllly wish he would come shower with me...I wonder if I should ask him to?*

"How are your eyes?" *Wow, that is quite possibly the most obvious come-on I could use...judges?*

"My right eye seems to be back to normal, my left is still a little blurry and I think the doctor was right that my color

119

vision seems off." Kane says reflectively, taking another huge bite of orange chicken. As he's chewing, I think he hears the question I was *really* asking, and his neck turns red as he glances at me and he swallows hard.

"My uh, close vision is pretty damn good…" he says roughly and he looks at me directly. I almost sway from the lack of blood to my brain as a rush of heat floods my southern hemisphere.

"Good, that's great," *I sound nervous, dammit.* "I'm so glad, um, so…I'm going to go, um, shower." *Ditzy and nervous, just shoot me now.* I'm almost sure Kane can read my mind because he gives me that sexy grin that makes my clit vibrate and I'm sure my cheeks are pinking up. *Well thank fuck, some of the blood decided to head north before I passed out.*

"Whoo, yeah, so…" I *giggle* and then want to throw myself out the window.

"Do you want me to wash your back?" Kane rumbles, standing and pulling his shirt off in that one smooth motion that is *so fucking hot.*

"God, yes," I gasp, and then seal my lips shut as he walks closer, leaning down to kiss me lightly as his fingers find the hem of my shirt. Lifting up my arms to be helpful, he smoothly pulls my shirt up over my head. I'm standing there in my bra and jeans. *You would think this was my first damn time, because I don't know what to do with my hands and I don't know why I'm so nervous. It's Kane. I've been dying to get closer to him since the moment I saw him.*

Kane turns and sits down on the edge of the bed, eyes on my face. He reaches out and hooks a finger in the waist of my jeans, right at the front, and slowly pulls me closer. I smile and let him, my eyes never leaving his.

He leans forward and kisses my stomach, goosebumps erupt everywhere and it's not from cold. He nuzzles my skin, his beard tickling deliciously and I tangle my fingers in his hair, pulling lightly. I feel his fingers at my waist and the button on my jeans is opened and he lays more kisses across my belly before looking up at me again.

My jeans slide down my hips as he tips his head back and I lean in and kiss him, hard, biting his lip lightly. He breaks the kiss with a groan and trails his lips down my neck as he helps me step out of my jeans. Sitting back, his eyes meet mine again as he reaches up and slowly pulls the band out of my hair. As it falls around my shoulders in a blonde waterfall, I reach behind my back and unhook my bra, letting the straps slide down my arms before tossing it to the side.

"You're so goddamn beautiful," Kane growls, his hands sliding up my side, his fingers on my ribs, his thumbs lightly stroke the sensitive underside of my breasts and I shiver.

"I want you," I whisper, and he groans again, his hands sliding down to my hips he nudges me back and stands. My hands trace his ink and the ridges and planes of his abs on their own accord. I lean forward and flick one of his nipples with my tongue. It hardens to a point and I reach for the button of his jeans, popping it open. I can feel him, hard and straining the denim, and I run my fingers up his length. His hips jerk once and his hands cup my face, tilting my head up as he kisses me.

I push his jeans and boxers off his hips slowly, as far as I can reach, and then he kicks them off. I feel the heat of him pinned against my stomach. Putting my hands on his chest, I push him backwards, and when he feels the bed behind his knees, he sits on the edge. Reaching for me, he slides my underwear off my hips, his eyes never leaving my face.

"Are you sure?" Kane asks, his face serious, and my heart almosts bursts and then settles for beating double time. Leaning down, I whisper in his ear.

"Baby, you promised to make me *scream.*" At my words, Kane growls and his hands are around my waist. I let out a squeal as he flips me onto my back on the bed, and then I moan because he buries his face between my thighs and his beard tickles every nerve ending and *ohmygod his tongue.* Hot and wet, I can feel him tasting me, and he teases my clit and then kisses the inside of my thigh and looks up at me. *Ohmygod, the heat in his eyes could make me burst into flames.*

Pushing up away from me, Kane stands and walks across the room. I am so damn distracted by *that* vision of perfection that I have to remind myself to keep my mouth from hanging open in dazed happiness. He reaches into his bag and comes back to the bed, rolling on a condom. *Be still my fucking heart.* Laying down beside me, he reaches for me, pulling me close, his hands in my hair as he kisses me long and deep.

I feel him pinned between us and I run my hands down my chest, reaching for him and letting him feel my fingers run up his length. He groans against my mouth as he rolls us, keeping me with him so that he ends up on his back with me on top. *Saddle up cowgirl, ohmygod.*

Leaning down, I kiss him again hard as I feel our bodies line up and I slide along him for a second before changing the angle and letting him drive in deep.

"Fuckkkk," I moan, and he grabs my hips, holding me still with his eyes shut as my own try to roll back in my head out of pure delight. Slowly, I start rocking my hips, looking down at him as his eyes open and he watches me. I move faster, his hands sliding up my ribs, so deliciously rough as his thumbs stroke my belly and brush my nipples.

Faster and faster I rock, feeling him match my rhythm, feeling that heavy swirl building in my belly. Faster, faster, and then his arms wrap around my waist and he pulls me down to his chest.

"Not yet," he growls, rolling us again. His arms are a cage of suede covered steel as he keeps his weight off me, looking deep into my eyes he leans in, kissing me hard. He kisses down my neck and sucks in one of my nipples, letting me feel his teeth as he drives into me again. Pushing up onto my elbows, the angle is perfect for me to see and feel every inch and it's all I can do not to throw my head back and orgasm on the spot. *Not yet, not yet, not yet.*

His body is amazing as he pistons his hips, grinding right over that bundle of nerves that makes me want to scream my pleasure. He leans down, sucking in my other nipple and lets me feel his teeth again, and then he kisses me hard, his hips pumping faster. *Not yet, not yet, not yet.*

A moan of pleasure that's close to a scream leaves my lips as Kane puts a hand behind the small of my back, holding it in an arch as he pounds into me, I feel my muscles clenching and I feel my legs shake, wanting to let go. *Not yet, not yet, not yet.*

"Kane…" I moan, louder this time, my hips start to rock, my core clenching as that heavy swirl in my gut is echoed in my head. I stare into his eyes.

"Come for me Wren," Kane's eyes are burning into mine, he speeds up even more, holding me tight. *Yes, yes, yes, yes, yes.*

"Kane!" I scream, and my head falls back. I stop breathing as the swirl overwhelms me and my eyes flutter shut. He drives into me, hard, again and again, and then falls off his own cliff as he yells my name.

An Old Coat

⚜

*K*ane

Wren is laying on her back, breath slowing, a fine sheen of sweat on her forehead as I brush her hair away from her face. My fingers continue a line along her cheek, down her neck, the valley between her breasts and trail lightly in a circle on her belly as I look at her. She smiles with her eyes closed, and sighs happily.

"You know...I think I might love you..." she says sleepily, her eyes still closed, and my heart stutters.

"Is that you or your southern nerve bundle talking?" I tease lightly, and her eyes open, finding mine as she giggles. Rolling up on her side to face me, her fingers trace the ink on my shoulder.

"Both, I took a quick poll," she says seriously, her eyes sparkling with laughter. Sliding my hand into her hair, I pull her to me, kissing her hard.

"I think I might love you too," I murmur against her lips and she pulls back to look at me, eyes bright. I stand up from the bed and hold out a hand. When she takes it, I pull her up with me and lead her to the shower.

* * *

Later, *much later, when the steam is so thick the mirror might never clear, and Wren's nails have marked my shoulders and I've brought her over the edge calling my name again,* she's sound asleep. Her blonde hair is tumbled all around her on the pillow, and she fell asleep smiling at me, her face content.

For whatever reason, my brain won't shut down and I can't sleep. Getting out of bed quietly, I look at the boxes on the floor by the window and decide to keep going through my old man's stuff.

Some of the things he kept mean nothing to me, old receipts that are too faded to read, ticket stubs to old fights, pictures of him in the arenas before and after fights with men and women I've never met. Random pieces of clothing, old jeans, gym t-shirts, old flannel shirts. I keep the pictures for now, I might try to figure out who some of the people in them are some day. The receipts and papers that are too faded to read, I throw in the trash. The clothes go in a pile, I'd put them in the trash too, but something tells me Wren will know how to find a place to donate them instead.

I pause and stare into the box for a moment when I find my old man's hunting jacket at the bottom. It's an old wool jacket, dark green with a flannel collar, and all kinds of pockets for gear when you're out in the woods. Lifting it out of the box, it still smells like the campfire that was blazing the last time I saw him wearing it, about a month after my mother died.

We'd gone out to this piece of farmland my mother had inherited, just outside of Gravity. There were two parcels, two hundred acres each, sitting next to each other near the river. One had gone to my aunt, the other to my mom. My aunt had sold hers when she left Gravity. At some point my old man sold my mother's off. He always needed money to fuel one of his binges out to Vegas to gamble and see the fights.

The day we went to the farm, we hiked all the way back to a tiny pond near some timber, and my old man had me find enough downed branches to build a fire. We sat and stared at the pond. We didn't talk much, I just fed the fire and he sat there, grieving. At the time I didn't know that's what he was doing, but as I got older I realized that, for him, that was the end.

Long after it got dark, we just laid there, on either side of the fire, staring up at the stars. When he spoke it surprised me, and I realized we'd been silent for hours.

"I kept your mama's ring, Kane." He said, gruffly. "I know sometimes I do stupid shit, so I'll tell you what I'm going to do with it...and then I hope I forget."

As he'd sat there in front of that fire, missing my mom and thinking, he'd worried a hole in the cuff of his old hunting coat. The next morning we got up, climbed in his old truck, and drove home. He walked right in the kitchen, got my mother's sewing box down from the cabinet, and sewed my mother's ring into the cuff. Then he handed me the coat.

"Go on, put this away," he'd said.

I took it and hung it deep in my own closet. For all the years I was with him, I managed to keep it hidden when he was looking for things to sell. More than once he took a swing at me and told me to go get it for him, said it didn't mean anything anymore. But I knew he didn't mean it, and I kept it hidden.

The last time I left him, I forgot the coat. I agonized over it, thought about tracking him down more than once, but I didn't want to find him and be disappointed. I'm almost afraid to look at the cuff now, ready to see the old seam ripped back open.

Turning it over, I find the sleeve and lift it up with a shaky hand. It's not torn, but it looks like he's sewed it again, the stitches are tiny, very neat. Setting it down for a minute I cross the room and grab a pocket knife out of my jeans. I carefully slit open the seam and hear the rustle of a piece of paper as my mother's ring falls out into my hand. *Son of a bitch...he kept it.*

Setting the coat down for a minute, I stare at the ring. It's an old family ring that belonged to my grandma, yellow gold, the band is so thin it looks like a piece of wire, but it's strong. A round diamond, maybe half carat, sits in six tall prongs.

My mother was so proud of that ring, she said back then yellow diamonds were rare, everyone wanted the fancy white ones, but her grandma's favorite color was yellow. My grandpa found her a perfect one at a jewelers in New York when he got back from the war. They got married a week later.

"When you know, you know," Mom had smiled at me, "that's just how love works, Kane." She'd loved my old man with everything she had, and she was his everything. He was good while she was alive. That fucking black ice on the bridge didn't just end her life that night...my old man may as well have died that day too.

My eyes are full of tears. My old man would have sucker-punched me and told me he was going to buy me a purse.

Wiping them away, I set the ring carefully on the table beside me and reach for the coat again. Pulling the cuff seam open wider, I pull out two folded pieces of paper. *That explains the new stitching.*

One of the papers has my name written on the outside. I open it first.

* * *

Kane,

I hope this old coat finds its way back to you. I hope I'm smart enough to give it to you if I ever see you again. I ripped the cuff open one night when I was on a bender. I was going to sell the damn thing, thought maybe it would get your Mama out of my head.

I sat there for hours, staring at it, long enough that I sobered up, put it back, and added something else that you should have someday.

Just in case, I pinned a note to it saying it should go to you, I didn't know who I'd be with, figured I'd be in hot water if I left a note for the wrong woman.

I know I ain't been the father you needed, I ain't been much of a man since your Mama died. I hope you find somebody someday you love as much as I loved her.

Dad-Ass Motherfucker

As I unfold the second paper, I can't blink fast enough to keep the fucking tears from rolling down my face.

It's the deed to the farm.

Only Good Surprises

~⚭⚬⚭~

W^{ren}

A choked sob wakes me up. I look around, disoriented. Kane is sitting in a chair by the window, a small lamp shines on the table beside him, and his face is in his hands. His shoulders are heaving as he cries silently. Getting up quietly, I walk around the bed and hug his head to my chest. His arms go around my waist and he crushes me to him. I feel his tears soaking through my t-shirt and my heart aches.

"Let it out, I've got you," I whisper, and we stay that way until his shoulders stop shaking. He silently hands me the papers, and as I read them, I glance at the table and see a ring sitting there. It's safe to say my opinion of Kane's father improves exponentially. I smile as I read the signature. The second paper Kane's father left appears to be the deed to some land.

"It's right outside of Gravity," Kane's voice is gravelly, quiet, as he sees me puzzling through the deed. "I thought he sold it

129

years ago."

"I'm glad the surprises your father left behind are good ones." I don't know what else to say. Kane looks up at me and smiles, so I think it was the right thing.

"Yeah, me too," he nods, standing. He takes a step closer to me and leans down, kissing me softly. Picking up the ring, the papers, and a small pile of pictures, he walks over to his bag, tucking them away. Almost as an afterthought it seems, he carefully folds up the hunting jacket and puts it in his bag too.

Reaching out, he takes my hand and leads me back to bed. Holding me close, I feel him kiss my hair.

"I love you, Wren," I hear him whisper, and my heart soars. I snuggle into his chest, lay a kiss on his neck, and go to sleep.

* * *

The next morning a weight has been lifted off of Kane's shoulders. He wakes me up, his beard tickling my neck as he kisses his way down my body, not stopping until he reaches my toes. A kiss and a tiny bite on the arch of my foot sends a shiver through me, and he looks up at me with *that* smile. In my head, I call it the, 'Just wait until you see what's next Baby', smile. *Oh boy.*

Rolling me over gently, Kane hooks a finger in each side of my underwear and pulls them off slowly. Crossing my arms under my head, I look over my shoulder at him as he runs a hand over my ass and whistles, making me laugh. He leans down and kisses my ankle, the back of my calf, the back of my thigh, *geez I hope I did a good job shaving back there.*

I feel his breath on my ass for just a moment before he kisses it and then gently lets me feel his teeth. My body reacts and I am *so hot for him.* My back arches, my ass sticking up in the air shamelessly, and I moan softly. Taking my *ever so subtle* cues, Kane does it again.

"I want you now," I gasp, I'm so ready, no more foreplay. Kane groans, his hand smoothing over my ass. I feel him moving on the bed and look over my shoulder at him as he reaches in his bag.

"Fuck," he mutters, opening the bag with both hands.

"Yes please," I sass back, and he grins at me, but then frowns.

"I'm going to run down to the hotel shop quick, I under-estimated us," he laughs. *Ohmygod, he's out of condoms...and adorable.*

"You can if you want to," I pause, a little unsure of how he'll react.

"Um...what?"

"If you feel better with one, that's fine, but I have an IUD, so I'm not going to get pregnant...it's okay with me if we don't use one." Kane drops his bag on the floor and turns, one hand grabbing my ass, and my laugh turns into a sigh of pleasure as his other hand winds into my hair. He pulls just hard enough to turn my head and kiss me, and I feel him, hard and ready, pressed against me.

I arch my back hard, pushing my ass into him, and he buries himself completely in one stroke with a groan. The very idea of quick and dirty with Kane flips my switch so fast that I already feel that heavy swirl building.

I'm pushing my hips back in rhythm with his thrusts, the slap of skin on skin cheering us on, Kane's strong hands gripping my hips. Slamming back one more time, I tip over the edge, my face buried in the sheets, body clenching. Kane's hands hold me steady as he pounds me through my orgasm. I feel him shudder behind me as he spills deep.

Kane lays down on the bed beside me as I flop onto my back, feeling like I have no control of my extremities, smiling like a cat that got the cream. *Oh unintended pun!*

"That was amazing," I wheeze out, still breathing hard.

"Yeah it was," Kane agrees, linking our fingers together, "every time with you is, Wren."

Swoon, swoon, swoon.

What Happens in Vegas

*K*ane

"So…we've never gone on a date," I walk up behind Wren as she brushes her hair. Her cheeks turn a beautiful pink and she just looks at me for a moment.

"Well, that's true…and funny considering the last couple of days," she laughs.

"I'm taking you on a date," I look at her in the mirror, and briefly consider tossing her back on the bed. I think she can read my mind because she laughs and walks across the room to grab her purse.

"I think we better leave now then," she giggles and swats me on the ass before scooting out the door.

We walk the strip, stopping for some fruity drink she wants to try and watch some street performers eat fire. We hold hands and wander, I buy her a little Vegas charm on a silver chain. Wren holds up her hair while I put it on her and then turns and kisses me.

Day turns into evening as we walk through the casinos, play a few hands of poker, try all the different foods and drinks she wants. No plans, just me and Wren together. We wander into what looks like a circus tent and the box office has two tickets for a show beginning in a few minutes.

Wren watches the show, I watch Wren. Her face lights up with delight at the acrobats and the theatrics. The entire show is designed to mimic a trip on Absinthe. I've never seen anything like it, and Wren claps and cheers when it's over. When we leave the tent she turns to me, devilish smile on her face.

"I'm ready for my first ink," she announces.

"Oh yeah?" I start counting how many drinks I think she might have had today, this is probably a bad idea.

"Yep! Let's do it, you can get one too!" She giggles, linking her arm through mine.

"Baby, no one in this town is touching your skin." Her eyes widen at my words.

"What? Why not?" She looks like she's not sure if she should be flattered or pouting. *She's tiny, I bet she's had too much.*

"Because," I gather her into my arms and kiss her, "you are perfect and not completely sober." Wren giggles, still not sure how to react. "If you still want one when we leave Vegas, I'll take you back in Georgia. We can both get something." *I would get anything she wanted, but sending up a little prayer she's not into unicorns or butterflies.*

"Oookaayyyy," Wren sighs, glancing around, "Oh! Five dollar tequila shots!"

* * *

A couple hours later, we're sitting at an outdoor cafe eating. Wren is giggling into a cheeseburger. I'm feeling that pleasant buzz that says I should probably stop drinking so that *one* of us keeps *both* of us out of trouble. The carbs are helping as I polish off my second burger and a mountain of fries.

"This has been...hands down...best date ever," Wren says, reaching across the table to boop me on the nose. I open my mouth to agree, but she gasps loudly before I speak.

"You know what would finish this day off perfect? Ohmygod, we should get married!"

Add Tequila to the 'Never Again' List

W^{ren}

"Could you stop the room please? I'd like to get off now." I feel like I'm on a terrible amusement park ride. Kane chuckles.

"Drink this, take these, eat this you'll feel better." I crack my eyes open and he's offering me a glass of water, ibuprofen and a banana.

"No thanks, I'm just going to let death take me." I close my eyes, willing death to take me.

"Baby you need to drink this," his voice is firmer, and his hands sit me up.

"No-oooo, death first." I'm whining. I know it. I don't fucking care.

The cup is at my lips. I drink the damn water. I take the pills. I eat the banana. I don't die.

"I'm sorry you have to see me like this…it's been a long time

136

since I didn't have to study or be at the hospital the next day...I guess I overdid it," *So I've rocketed past wishing for death, and I'm at the remorse and apologies stage of my hangover. At this rate I'll get through the embarrassing memories, check my phone for drunk calls and texts and be good to go by noon.*

"What time is it?" Struggling to sit up, I glance at my phone. Two in the afternoon. *Well that's just great.*

Rolling out of bed, Kane's hands stop me from landing in a heap on the floor, and I smile at him as I shake him off and stumble towards the bathroom. Feeling almost human again after I pee, I grab my toothbrush, determined to get rid of the feeling that something died in my mouth while I was sleeping.

Standing at the mirror as I brush my teeth, I'm happy to see that my hair has not been cut, *after the super unfortunate 'bangs' incident where I swore off Sangria forever,* my makeup is not smeared everywhere, and I do not seem to have vomited. Spitting out the toothpaste, I rinse and then put the toothbrush away, admiring Kane's ring twinkling on my left hand.

...the fuck. ...ohmygod. Feeling like I just wandered back to the wishing for death stage, my stomach rolls and I put both hands on the counter and press my forehead to the cool mirror until the nausea passes.

Ohmygod, I think I got married last night. I even remember suggesting it as a super-amazing plan. Ohmygod.

Walking slowly out of the bathroom, Kane is sitting on the bed, his back propped up on the headboard with pillows, watching an old movie. He glances at me and pushes the remote button to turn off the TV.

"Feeling better?" He stretches and stands up walking over and putting his arms around me.

Heart: Seriously, would marrying Kane actually be the dumbest thing I ever did? I mean that's at least a distant third after the Sangria bangs and any interaction EVER with Bradley, right?

Brain: Do you hear yourself? You got married, drunk, in Vegas. You are a cliche.

Heart: Maybe I just got to act on what I really wanted to do, for once, instead of listening to YOU.

Brain: WHAT ARE YOU TALKING ABOUT? YOU NEVER LISTEN TO ME!

Heart: Well I'm listening to you complain right now, aren't I? And why? Because we MAYBE got married to someone AMAZING. Sheesh.

Putting my arms around his waist I breathe him in, trying to actually be upset that I might have drunkenly married this man last night. I can't. I am pretty sure being married to Kane *would* be amazing. I am pretty sure that, while I should probably date him for a while, learn his favorite color and favorite food and… birthday…middle name…*okay there's a lot*, none of those things would change how I'm feeling about him. *Diagnosis...L-U-V. Dammit, Jenna was right.*

"So…how much of last night do you remember?" Kane's voice rumbles through his chest. Leaning back, I look up at him. His jaw is set, face serious. *Uh oh.*

"Well, that Absinthe show was insanely cool, and I'm pretty sure you wouldn't let me get a tattoo…" *deep breath,* "and I think…maybe…I proposed marriage…and I woke up with this on." My voice only trembles a little, at the end, as I step back from Kane and hold up my left hand between us. Kane smiles down at my hand and then looks into my eyes.

"That's pretty accurate…yes," he murmurs. "Except we didn't

get married." At his words, I let out a breath I didn't realize I was holding.

Brain: Well thank fuck...I think...
  Heart: Dang it.

"Oh! We didn't, oh well, that's good, phew!" *Cue over-the-top sweat wipe off to demonstrate how 'phew' the situation is, god I'm an idiot.* "I mean, not that it would have been the *worst* thing..." *I really need to stop talking.* "So, um..." I hurriedly fill the silence, "why am I wearing this ring?" Kane laughs.

"Well, last night you were pretty sure a Vegas wedding was your absolute dream, so I talked you into coming back to the hotel to pick up the ring." His eyes slide away from my face, remembering and his look is soft.

"You got on one knee and proposed to me, and then had me do the same for you," Kane glances at me, reddening at the next bit. "And then you chased me around the room for a while, and I finally tucked you in pouting because we didn't have sex again." He smiles when I burst into nervous giggles.

"I am so sorry, Kane," *What a righteous pain in the ass I was... tequila is now on the do-not-drink-ever-again list with Sangria.*

"Well, mostly you just tested my willpower," Kane laughs, "I'd had enough to drink too...I almost let you talk me into pretty much everything."

"Well, you've got to admit...it was a pretty good list," I tease, feeling better. We're okay. I got drunk and annoying, but we're okay. Slipping the ring off, I hold it out to him. He takes it carefully, not smiling anymore.

"Thank you for that," I say lightly.

"It looked good on you," he whispers, turning to put it in his bag.

Getting My Head Straight

*K*ane

The second she took that ring off, I wanted to get down on one knee and ask her to put it back on her finger. It's crazy, I know that, but waking up and seeing Wren wearing that ring made me wish it was real. *I swear she seemed disappointed too...*

"I'm starving," Wren announces, flopping on the bed beside me.

"Do you want to go out or do you want to take another nap while I go get something?" I know the answer as soon as I say it because she smiles and burrows under the covers.

"You are an *angel* Kane. One little nap and I'll be right as rain, we can go out again tonight if you want, I'll skip the tequila shots, I promise," her soft voice lights my heart on fire and I reach down, smoothing the tangles of her hair away from her face.

"It's a date, back soon." She smiles at me and closes her eyes to sleep. Grabbing my wallet and a room key, I leave quietly.

I decide to walk a little, give her time to nap, give me time to think. A big part of me wants to shoot for happily ever after. I want to go back to Georgia with Wren, I want to build a home and a life with her, on the land my parents gave me. I want her to finish her residency and become a doctor. I want her to have my babies, as many as she wants. I want it all.

But there's a tiny little piece of my soul that won't stop jabbing me. She's going to be a doctor. She has an amazing future ahead of her, and she doesn't need me, or the problems I can't seem to shake. I keep walking, my mood dark, thinking, trying to decide if I'm right for Wren. No matter how bad I want the answer to be yes, I think it's no.

Maybe all of this has just moved too fast for both of us. I don't want Wren to be with me just because she got caught up in taking care of me and thinks she feels more. Maybe we just need to slow things down…maybe when we get back, I'll let her go on ahead to Georgia and stay in Texas for a few weeks, tying up loose ends. See if she still wants me around after she's had some space.

Feeling resolved, I glance around, realizing that I haven't been paying attention to anything while I've been walking and it's getting late. Getting my bearings, I stop at the smoothie shop she liked yesterday and get her one with no booze added. Heading back to the hotel, I stop in and buy two pizzas at the little pizzeria off the lobby and take the elevator up to our room.

A Quick Exit

Wren

I'm just getting to sleep when I hear a buzzing noise in the covers. Kane must have forgotten his phone, mine plays a tinkly little song. Pawing through the covers with a sigh, I find it and look blearily at the screen. There's a missed call, and then several texts popped through, one after the other.

Joe: Hey, we've got a problem.

Joe: Some guys showed up at the bar, laid into Troy pretty good, trying to find you.

Joe: Troy didn't have your number, didn't know where you were. So they left a message, from someone named Smitty.

Joe: They said he'll be waiting to hear from you when you get back to Texas, said you get a week to deal with your old man's shit and then you'll bring back what's his.

Joe: What's this all about? You in some trouble?

143

Joe: Call me.

My hangover disappears as a shiver runs up the backs of my arms. I waited too long to tell Kane my secret, and now it's too late. Jumping out of bed, I hurriedly pack all of my things. Finding the hotel stationary in the desk, I leave him a note that doesn't really explain anything. Swiping Kane's phone open, I delete the call and texts from Joe. Tears filling my eyes, I look around the room, and walking over to his bag I steal one of his t-shirts, stuffing it in my purse. I leave the keys to his truck on the table, along with my note.

Walking quickly out the door and down the hall to the elevator, I leave the hotel and hail a cab. I put my brain on auto-pilot as I book a flight, find my gate, and board the plane. Landing in Texas, my phone immediately lights up with missed calls, all from Kane.

I get another cab to Kane's apartment and pick up my car. I don't stop at my place, I don't have time. Sitting in my car in the alley behind Kane's apartment, I look at my phone again.

Kane: Where are you?
  Kane: I got your note, don't leave like this.
  Kane: Baby, we can figure out whatever this is, talk to me.
  Kane: I love you.

A little sob escapes me, I don't want to hurt him, but this is for me to finish. Heading east, I drive into the night. I have to fix this for us, the only person I call is Gran.

Radio Silence

*K*ane

Sitting on the edge of the bed in the hotel, I stare at Wren's note.

Kane,

I had to go. There is something that I should have told you, it was almost too late when I figured it out, but I can fix everything. I hope you can trust me. I'm not trying to be cryptic, it's just a lot, too much for me to write on this paper. I hope you will let me tell you everything the next time I see you.

Please meet me at my Gran's house in Gravity in a week. I won't blame you if you decide I'm a righteous pain in the ass and stay in Texas.

I love you. I hope you remember that when I tell you the rest.

Wren

It doesn't help to read the note over, but I don't know what else to do. I have no idea what happened. I don't know what she figured out and what she's going to fix. All I know is, she left, she's not answering her phone, I'm stuck here until tomorrow, and the pizza is getting cold. I can only solve one of those problems tonight.

The Heart-Brain War

W^{ren}

Stopping at a truck stop on the border of east Texas, I order a huge breakfast and then smile at the plate, thinking of Kane. *He could eat three of these.* I'm sure he's confused and angry, but I'll explain everything in Gravity.

One week. I need to fix what I can, and then I need to get my head on straight about Kane. I need to figure out if I just fell in head over heels because he was hurt and needed me…or if this is the real deal. My heart and my brain are at war.

Brain: Time and space will tell her everything, she needs to take a minute.

Heart: Fuck off. Stop this nonsense. She should call him.

Brain: She can handle herself, she needs to make sure she's not rushing into anything with him.

Heart: Fuck off. Call him, ask him to come find her.

Brain: She can't do that, she'll see him in a week, if he doesn't come it wasn't real.

Heart: FUCK OFF. Call him, ask him for the ring back.

Brain: Sigh...it's like dealing with a drunk raccoon, talking to you.

Heart: FUCK OFF.

Brain: I rest my case.

Turning on my phone's GPS, I look up the address. Wolfing down the rest of my breakfast, I pay the bill and get back in my car. I've got a lot of driving ahead of me before the day is done.

Pulling into a tiny motel in eastern Louisiana, I decide to get some sleep, tomorrow is going to be an interesting day. The bed feels big and cold, I miss Kane. I don't let myself even glance at my phone.

I have to fix this first.

* * *

Waking up the next morning, I shower and get ready as if I'm preparing for battle. Forcing myself to go have some breakfast at a cafe attached to the motel, I finally get on the road, this time heading south. I feel like I've got an angry swarm of wasps in my stomach trying to get out.

Three hours later, I pull up outside the bar, a faded sign above the door says 'Smitty's Place'. I sit in the car for another minute, just breathing. *Six minutes. I sat and breathed for six minutes.*

Finally, taking a deep breath, I get out of the car, walk up to the door and push it open. Taking a few steps in, I let my eyes adjust to the dim light and look around. It's two in the afternoon, so the bar is pretty empty, a couple of guys are bellied up to the bar at the left and a few people are eating burgers in a booth. Everyone glances at me when I walk in, but they all turn back to their food and beer, uninterested.

"You lost, Honey?" The bartender is wiping the counter with a dirty rag, toothpick poking out the side of his mouth.

"No, I'm looking for Smitty." I wish my voice sounded more confident, but I'm not. This might be the worst idea I've had in a long time.

"You don't look tough enough to waitress here, but I'll let him decide, he's in the back." The bartender scoffs, shaking his head. He goes back to cleaning the counter, dismissing me. I don't bother to correct him, I just walk to the back of the bar and down a narrow hall. I pass a couple of doors, bathrooms and then what looks like a couple of storage rooms. Straight back there's a door with a window that says, 'Office'. I can see the edge of a desk and a lamp glowing. Taking a deep breath I knock on the door.

"What?" A gruff voice hollers from inside, "Dammit Steve, quit knocking and get in here, I ain't the President." I smile a tiny bit in spite of myself, but smooth my face into indifference and open the door.

The man behind the desk doesn't look up as he scribbles on a yellow legal pad. Thick, dark grey hair is carefully combed back and he's wearing a denim shirt. Pulling reading glasses off his nose, he sighs and looks up, startling when I'm not Steve.

"You lost?" He's got that gravelly voice of a man who spent his life in bars before the smoking ban.

"Not if you're Smitty." Taking a couple of steps into the office, I close the door behind me.

"Fine, I'll bite, who the hell are you?" He narrows his eyes, looking me over carefully. I pull a heavy gold ring out of my pocket and set it on his desk. His eyes widen, staring at the ring.

"Where in hell did you get that?" He can't decide whether to look at me or the ring. Finally, reaching out, he picks it up, turning it over and staring at the crest on the top.

"If I were being formal, I would call you Jerick Smythe Donovan," I say carefully, looking him right in the eye. "Hello, Dad."

Missed Call

⸻❧⸻

*K*ane

I wake up and Wren's still gone. I glance at my phone, radio silence. I don't really feel much, just helpless, and it pisses me off. I laid awake a long time last night, trying to figure out what exactly made her run off. In her note, she said she could fix everything. The only problem I've got is Smitty looming out there in Louisiana, but she wouldn't have any idea where to even *find* him, so that doesn't make sense.

Going through the motions, I shower and get dressed and pack all my shit. I look through the boxes one more time and then just fold them shut and leave them behind. I've got the ring and the deed to the land zipped into a pocket in my duffle bag. Checking out of the hotel, I head for the funeral home.

Releasing my dad's remains is a pretty simple process.

"Ronald Anderson, Mr. Morgan," the funeral director's hand is cold and dry as he shakes mine quickly. "Might I show you the exclusive collection of urns and vessels we have that will respectfully house your loved one on a mantle or other place of honor in your home?"

"No, and I'm not interested in a lengthy sales pitch." Ron looks taken aback at my tone.

"Understood, Mr. Morgan, and might I offer you our services for a memorial cele-" I cut him off.

"No, just the ashes, Ron, I've got a long trip home." My patience is wire thin, and I think Ron can tell.

"A moment please, Mr. Morgan," he says coldly, disappearing into the back of the building. Several minutes later he walks back out, handing me some paperwork. I sign the papers and hand him a wad of cash. He takes both and disappears again, returning almost immediately with a small cardboard box.

"A...pleasure, Mr. Morgan." He smiles thinly and disappears into the back room again, leaving me to see myself out.

* * *

My eyes are good enough for me to drive home from the airport, and Wren left my truck keys behind. I pull into the alley behind my apartment and just sit there, deciding what to do. My plan to give her some space is a shit plan. I don't want to do that anymore. Walking up the stairs to my apartment, I look around. Grabbing a beer out of the fridge, I sit on the couch, listening to music, drinking, wondering where Wren is and what she's doing.

Fuck it. Setting the beer on the counter, I walk in the laundry room. I've got a stack of those plastic storage tubs. It takes me three hours to pack up what I want from the apartment. I seatbelt the aloe plant in the passenger side, leave the keys on the counter. Phone call to the landlord telling him he can keep the deposit and I'm back on the road.

Walking into Joe's bar, able to see again, feels good. Troy is on the door, and his smile is broad when I park my truck.

"Jesus Kane, it's good to see you man, those are some wicked scars," he's happy to see me and I know he means it as a compliment, but I tense up a little.

"Thanks Troy, good to be back." My eyebrow has a little line where it won't grow, and my eyelashes came back in pure white where the stitches were. There's another little blaze scar on my cheekbone. The rest you can't really see, except for a big one on my shoulder that went through some ink and wrinkled the linework.

"You gonna start working again soon?" Troy's voice is hopeful, and I grin at him, knowing he'd rather I came back and handled the rowdy crews on the weekends, like I used to do every Friday and Saturday night. *Before Wren walked into this bar and shook my world like a birthday card.*

"No, I came to say goodbye. I'm heading back to Georgia." I hold out my hand as Troy's face falls, disappointed.

"Well that's a damn shame. Good luck man," he shakes my hand firmly and claps me on the shoulder. I nod and walk in the bar. Joe is stacking glasses carefully on the shelf as I walk up.

"How about a beer, Joe?" I ask, loud enough to be heard. It's pretty early yet, so the bar isn't packed, just a moderate crowd. Joe turns to me, smiling.

"Hell yeah, I'll have a beer," he laughs, cracking open a bottle for each of us and tipping his at me in a toast before taking a swig. He looks at me carefully and nods.

"You look good. You get my messages about the guys that stopped by the other night?" He asks gravely. *Shit.*

"I didn't get any messages, who stopped by?" I've got a bad feeling in my gut that it's the same ones who were in my apartment. Joe pulls his phone out and taps the screen.

"Is this your number? I thought I sent it right. I hate fucking texting, but you didn't answer when I called," Joe grumbles, showing me his phone. It's my number and my heart sinks as I see that he called and texted a bunch of times the other night... right before Wren left...the night I left my phone behind. Fear sears through my gut. She is in over her head if she thinks she can fix things with Smitty.

"Thanks for everything Joe, I can't stay." I reach over the bar and pull him into a one-armed hug.

"Stop back sometime, hear?" Joe says by way of goodbye, tipping his beer at me one more time. I nod, walk out the door, wave at Troy and jump in my truck. *How in the hell would Wren go find Smitty? Who would she know that could point her to his bar?* I hope I'm worrying over nothing, but none of this makes sense, I need to find her, now.

Calling her phone, it goes straight to voicemail, I hang up without leaving a message, and drive faster.

There's Got to be a Price

W^{ren}

"Wren?" Smitty's hoarse whisper seems loud in the silence that follows my greeting.

"Yeah, it's me." I stare at him hard, trying to feel something for this man that my mother loved and married. The man my Gran loves so much she can't talk about, and feels so guilty about that she keeps caring for his wife. I've got a lot of explaining to do when I get home, the phone call was hard.

"Gran, I need you to tell me how to find my father." There was no easy way to say it, best to just say it.

"Why on earth would you need to find him," Gran gasped, and her usually strong voice began to shake, "after all these years, girl, why?"

"He and I need to talk, I can't tell you any more than that right now, Gran. I'll explain it when I get home."

She'd thrown out a few more excuses, but I held firm and

she gave me an address.

"What are you doing here?" Smitty is staring at me like an oasis in the desert, "Is your Gran with you...or...your mom?"

"No." My voice is so harsh, but I can't forgive everything.

It's been more than 20 years, but this man got drunk one night and my mother tried to help him to bed. He shoved her away, cursing, and she fell, hitting her head on the edge of a heavy oak nightstand. I was standing in the doorway, his yelling had woken me up, and I watched the blood soak her beautiful blonde hair. Scared sober as soon as he realized she was hurt, he'd immediately called an ambulance, and my Gran, but the damage was done.

The next few days had been quiet at my house. My dad and my Gran took turns at the hospital, and one early morning I heard them talking quietly in the kitchen, thinking I was still asleep. My room was upstairs and I crept out onto the top stair so that I could see them in the kitchen.

"I'm not going to tell the police you caused this," my Gran's voice was as cold as I'd ever heard it, "but you are going to leave. You're going to leave and let me raise this child and care for her mother. You're going to send money, but you're not coming back. That little girl doesn't need you." Her voice had broken at the end, but she'd stood firm. My father sat there, head in his hands, saying nothing. My Gran had sat there quiet for a few minutes, the silence building until she took a deep breath.

"You go by Jerick Smythe from now on, hear?" Her voice was hoarse as she disowned her own son. "You hurt the woman you loved and stole that little girl's mama away from her, she ain't never going to be the same. There's got to be a price for that. You're not fit to carry your father's name," she finished with a whisper.

I'd sat on those stairs a long time after he got up, packed a bag, and walked out the door, listening to my Gran cry.

* * *

"I'm not sure which was worse," I whisper, "hearing Gran tell you to get out of my life, or knowing for more than twenty years now that you gave me up that easy." His head swings up, staring at me, his eyes full of tears.

"I hurt the woman I was supposed to take care of," he says roughly, "there's a price for that."

"Doesn't seem fair that I had to pay too," I can't do anything but whisper, "I was too young, I needed you. I grew up listening to people whisper that my dad walked out because my mom tripped and hit her head and it scrambled her brain," my voice gives out. I stop, sucking in a shuddering breath as I fight the tears back.

"I didn't know what to do," Jerick mutters, "I'd ruined everything in one stupid fucking night. I've been paying ever since."

"Yes, and look at you now…king of this bar, illegal gambling operations, loan shark and then roughing up people when they don't pay, what a *pillar* of the community you've become, trying to pay your *penance*." I spit the words, every fiber of my being disappointed in this man that I can barely remember.

"How do you know about all that?" He stares at me, glancing down at the ring he still holds in his hand.

"Yeah, I see you doing the math." I sneer, unable to stop myself, feeling more anger than I expected come pouring out now that it has a target. "Kane Morgan is mine. Do you hear me? His father is dead, you've got grandad's ring back, and you are going to drop whatever this was, it's *done*." My chest is heaving, I don't remember standing up, and I realize I've been yelling. Jerick is still staring at me. I sit down heavily.

That night at Crystal's when I held out my hand to take those pictures, I'd opened the dresser drawer to put them in a safe spot. There sat this big gold ring, on a pile of lacy underwear, gleaming in the dim light of the room. I recognized it immediately, my Grandad wore it everyday until he died. I remember how important it was to my father when my Gran gave it to him after Grandad's funeral.

"It's done," he whispers, nodding. "Anything you want, Wren. There's not a damn thing I can do to make things up to you. Someday you'll just have to dance on my grave, because I've got nothing you want." He reaches out and sets the ring on the desk, close to me. "I don't deserve that ring, you should have it." He puts his head in his hands just like he did twenty years ago before he walked out of my life.

"Look at me you fucking pansy," I grit out, and his head snaps up, "you think you've paid? Bullshit, you ran the fuck away. You ran away and did nothing good. You owe me, and you owe Ma, and here's what you're going to do."

Bygones

Kane

I finally have to stop and get some sleep, my eyes are getting halos so bad that I'm afraid I'm going to wreck my damn truck. I nap at a rest stop for a couple hours and get back on the road, hoping I'm not too late, hoping Wren couldn't find him. As my truck roars into town, I barely throw it in park and turn it off before I jump out and shoulder open the door to Smitty's bar.

The bar is empty except for Smitty, and the bartender, Steve. Smitty sees me and sighs. Jerking his head at Steve, who quickly leaves us alone, heading out for a smoke, Smitty turns to me.

"She's not here." He says gruffly. Turning back to the counter he picks something up and turns to me, holding out his hand so that I can see the ring laying on his palm.

"Did she bring you that?" I ask, knowing that she must have found it at Crystal's that night.

"She did," Smitty gives a low laugh, "chewed my ass off too."

"How did she find you?" I can't piece all this together, it just doesn't make any sense.

"Her Gran knew where I was," Smitty grunts, "must have cost her dear to tell Wren where to find me," he gets up and walks around the end of the bar. I hear the cooler doors open and slam and he turns, setting two beers on the counter. Popping the cap off one he sets it on the counter and nods at it, indicating it's for me. He pops the cap off the other and takes a drink.

"Her Gran knew where I was..." Fucking hell, Smitty is Wren's father. I walk over to the bar and take the beer, the cold against my hand snaps me out of the shock. I stare at Smitty for a minute, piecing it all together.

"Yeah," Smitty grunts, knowing that I've figured it out. We drink in silence for a minute.

"Where do we go from here?" I ask cautiously, I'm in uncharted waters.

"Wren told me what I've got to do," Smitty snorts. "*You* get yer ass to Georgia and take care of Wren. You better believe if you ever let her down as bad as I did…things will end a little different than they are today." He gives me a hard look.

"I'll be there as long as she'll have me," I mean every word.

"Oh, she'll have you, I got the distinct impression she would've hamstrung me if I hadn't agreed to let bygones be bygones." Smitty shakes his head, a look of pride on his face. "Said you belong to her, so all I'm going to say is good luck. She…reminds me of her mother." His eyes are suspiciously shiny as he turns and takes a swig of beer. He doesn't look at me again as I walk out of the bar.

I Think I Might Love You

W^ren

I didn't go to Gravity when I left Louisiana.

I went back to Texas. I wasn't ready to face my Gran, I wasn't sure I'd made the right decision about my father. I needed to think. So I went back to Texas and rented a truck and packed up my apartment. I finally plugged my phone in, it'd been dead for more than a day, and I called Gran first.

"Wren, you scared the devil out of me! Why didn't you call back!" I can hear the tears in her voice, and I feel awful.

"Gran, my phone died and I lost my charger somewhere. I'm back in Texas, but I'm going to pack up and come home, okay?" It's too much to tell her over the phone.

"Did you see him, Wren?" Her voice is stronger, she's trying so hard to hide her emotions.

"Yes Gran, I saw him."

"How was he?" Her voice is full of hope. No matter what,

he's her son. I just hope I'm doing the right thing.

"He was glad to see me, Gran. You and I have a lot to talk about when I get home."

"Alright honey, you be careful. I'll see you soon." She waits to hear me agree and disconnects.

I pack all day and bribe the neighbor guys with the case of beer in my fridge and two pizzas from the freezer to do the heavy lifting. By the time the sun sets, the truck is full. I camp in the living room for my last night in Texas. Tomorrow I'll go pick Max up and we're heading for Georgia.

Finally, I settle my nerves and call Kane. He doesn't answer, and my stomach gives a little heave of disappointment. I wanted to hear his voice. This has been such a mess and I just want to talk to him, make him understand everything. *What if he hates me for who my father is?* The thought skitters across my brain, not for the first time, but this time I can't shake the feeling that maybe this is too much. As I'm laying there, staring at the ceiling, waiting for sleep that is eluding me, my phone rings.

"Kane," I breathe, afraid he's going to yell at me or just hang up once he knows I'm okay, or just be indifferent.

"Baby you scared me," he growls into the phone and every last one of my nerve endings curls up and explodes with joy. *One well-placed 'Baby' and I get goosebumps in my hair for fuckssake.*

"I know, and I'm sorry, *so* sorry, Kane," I whisper. I don't know what else to say. 'Sorry my dad's an asshole that was kind of ruining your life' isn't the direction I want to go right now. "I gave the ring to Smitty."

"I know, I managed to follow you that far," Kane says softly. "Where are you?" He asks, and I melt a little that he's not going to yell at me.

"Laying in my empty living room in Texas. I packed up my apartment. I'm picking up Max and coming home, I'll be there the day after tomorrow." I'm holding the phone against my cheek hard enough that I notice the pain, trying to get closer to him.

"I got into Gravity just a little while ago. I'm going to go out and look at the land my parents left me tomorrow." Kane pauses, and I just wait, I don't want him to stop talking. "I'm going to start looking for a place to live for now, but if I remember right, there's a pond and a little timber," he pauses again, blowing out a shaky breath. "The last good memories I have of my father are by that pond, I think I'd like to build a house there."

At this point I feel like we've skirted around the 'where are we at' question long enough, and I can't stand it anymore.

"Will you build a house big enough for both of us?" I ask quietly, smiling hopefully when I hear him suck in a quick breath.

"As big as you want, Wren," his voice is soft and relieved, and that's all I need to hear.

"I think I might love you," I whisper.

"I think I might love you too," he whispers back.

Jenna has a special suitcase packed and ready to go for Max when I arrive the next morning.

"It's just a few things, he got a little bored, and I felt like he needed some outfits...shut up, stop laughing!" Jenna squawks defensively when she hands it to me. She 'adores' the earrings, putting them in immediately, and asks how everything turned out in Vegas. I end up just saying, 'fine'. It's too much to share, hell *I'm* still wrapping my head around parts of the last week.

With a final hug and a blown kiss at Max, Jenna steps back and lets me load him into the cab of the truck. I wave goodbye for both of us as we point the truck east and head for home.

Skinnydipping

Kane

I'm out at the farm when Wren gets back to Gravity. I see her little car driving slowly along the road and then she parks and gets out. She walks towards me across the field, hair shining in the sunlight, smiling. I'm about ready to break into a run like they do in the movies. But then I think, for a split second, what that would look like, and just walk fast.

She runs the last twenty feet or so, *it is the textbook definition of cute,* and jumps into my arms. Wrapping her legs around my waist, she buries her face in my neck and I feel tears soaking into my shirt. I lean back a little, trying to see her face, but she bites my shoulder and then hugs me tighter when I laugh.

We stand that way for a long time, and finally, she unwraps her legs from around my waist and I set her down.

"I'm sorry," she mumbles, looking away and wiping her eyes. Taking her face in both my hands, I use my thumbs to wipe

165

away the rest of her tears and kiss her. *Really* kiss her. When we finally stop to suck in a breath, I take her hand and walk her to the pond. We talk about everything that's happened since she left me in Las Vegas.

We talk about the future more than the past, and sitting in the back of my truck, we watch the sun set. The lightning bugs come out, the moon is bright, and Wren looks around happily.

"You know, I could get used to living in the country," she pulls her shirt off, lays back in the truck bed and shimmies out of her shorts.

"*I'm* going to love living in the country if you're planning to walk around naked all the time," I agree.

Wren laughs and walks to the edge of the pond, dipping her toes in the water. There's a gravelly patch of sand that forms a natural little beach, most of the rest of the pond has tall grass swaying around the edge. Turning she crooks a teasing finger in my direction. Pulling my shirt off and kicking off my boots, I unbutton my jeans as I walk to the edge of the pond, pulling her close.

She pushes my jeans and boxers off my hips as my lips find hers. I reach behind her and unhook her bra, feeling her nipples pebble against my chest as I slide the straps off her shoulders and toss it to the side. I feel her shift as she kicks off her underwear. The pond is warmer than the night air after the bright sunshine of the day. I lead Wren deeper into the water and she wraps her arms around my neck.

We swim and kiss and talk, and when we get tired, I unroll a couple of sleeping bags in the bed of my truck and we lay together under the stars, music playing softly on the radio.

Rolling on her side to face me, Wren tilts her head up for a kiss. Her lips leave mine and she kisses down my neck, biting me softly at the collar bone. I can't stop the groan from escaping my lips and she looks up at me with a smile as she works her way down my stomach.

When I feel her lips wrap around me, I tangle my fingers in her hair and hold her still. She hums with delight and pulls against my hand, taking me deeper into her mouth. Letting go of her hair, I lean up on my elbows and watch her. She looks up at me as her lips tease the ridge, and then she takes me deep again. Her fingers squeeze gently and I lay back, feeling the weight building in my stomach, wanting this to last forever.

Wren kisses her way back up my stomach, I feel her nipples against my chest and then she straddles me, sliding along my length. She's hot and wet, and I close my eyes for a minute to regain control. When I feel her fingers wrap around my cock to guide me in, I thrust hard and hear her gasp with delight.

"Hard, Kane," she moans, and I roll us so that I'm above her, holding my weight in my arms and her legs are wrapped around my waist. Thrusting hard, I pound her, loving the sounds she makes when I'm buried deep inside her body. I feel her body start to tighten around me and speed up. Her eyes fly open and find mine. I kiss her lips and then dip my head down and suck in one of her nipples. She moans again, louder, back arching to meet me.

Shifting back so that I'm sitting on my knees, I lift her up, facing me. She smiles with delight at the new angle, her arms wrap around my neck and she shifts, watching my face.

"Ride, Baby," I growl and her eyes roll back as her hips rock, grinding until I'm as deep as I can be in her body. She rolls her hips, forward and back, fast, over and over, and suddenly I'm ready to lose control. I start to grip her hip with one hand to slow her down, make it last. She kisses me quickly and then looks into my eyes.

"Come for me Kane," she whispers. I let go of her hip and let her ride as hard as she wants. The wave crashes over me and I feel her clenching tight around me. I let go as she screams her pleasure to the stars.

All's Well That Ends Well

Wren

My father came to Gravity two months after we arrived. We'd talked on the phone, and I'd had a chance to talk it over with Gran. We decided the time was right. Ma is out on the front porch, sitting in a rocker enjoying a lemonade when he pulls up. Gran and I are in the kitchen, but glance at each other and silently decide not to go outside right away.

He sits in his truck for a solid minute before the door opens, probably gathering his courage. As he walks up the sidewalk, Ma looks at him carefully.

"Jerick, honey," she says, as if not a day has gone by, "when did all your hair turn grey?" He lets out a low cry and falls to his knees in front of her, his arms wrapping around her waist. She strokes his hair and murmurs 'it's okay', over and over until his shoulders stop heaving, and calmly invites him to dinner.

169

"Maybe he's paid enough," Gran looks at me, a single tear trickling down her cheek.

"Maybe he needs to pay her with love and care," I whisper. "I made him sell everything off and shut everything down in Louisiana. He's going to be here, where she needs him." He agreed to every term I laid down, and he gets nothing in return but a chance to prove that he can be better.

* * *

We're staying in an apartment downtown. I went out to Tyler farms and visited Veronica a couple of days after we arrived, and when she heard we were staying in a hotel, she offered us the third floor apartment of her office downtown.

"I'm doing all of my work from home these days," she smiled, one hand on her very pregnant belly as she fondly watched her husband, Shane, scoop up their toddler and ride him around on his shoulders. "It's yours for as long as you need it." She asked about school and my residency, a speculative gleam entering her eyes.

"If you're going to be here long-term, it's never too early to start thinking about a rural hospital...mmmhmmm, maybe we could add in a specialty component that supports the company..." she'd pulled her phone out, dictating notes as she thought of them, letting me stand there in stunned silence as she planned out my dream job.

The Very Best Date

W*ren*

Arriving at the airport, I clap my hands like a silly girl when I see that we're going back to Las Vegas.

"I don't know if you can top our first date there," I tease as he pulls me into his side, kissing my hair.

"I'll take that bet," he rumbles, smiling at me.

We stay at the Mirage, we walk the strip and get fruity drinks. We get tickets to the Absinthe show and it is even more amazing when I've only had a couple of drinks and *no* tequila shots. As we walk the strip after the show, Kane stops in front of a tattoo parlor.

"Are you ready?" He asks, "It's okay if you're not, but I checked this place out, just in case you were serious."

"Absolutely! We're getting butterflies!" I crow with delight and then fall into his arms laughing at the look on his face.

"Actually I have thought about it," I admit once we've both

stopped laughing, "and I have an idea."

Two hours later, I can not stop staring at the beautiful lightbulb inked into the skin on the left side of my ribcage. *Literally can't stop staring, walking around with my shirt pulled up to just short of scandalous.*

Kane has one too. When I told him that's what I wanted to get, he just looked at me for a moment and then he smiled.

"Because they *shine*," he murmured, "perfect."

The next morning, *fine, afternoon, I tackled Kane and climbed him like a damn tree, we spent the morning in bed,* Kane looks at me seriously.

"Ready for one last stop on our date?" He asks gravely.

"Yes, but you don't look like it will be very fun," I tease, and he smiles.

"I think it might be the best part yet, actually. The itinerary is on the desk if you want to see." He says casually. My curiosity piqued, I walk over and open the envelope. There's one piece of paper inside. I unfold it as I turn around and see an official-looking seal at the top of the paper.

"Is this a-ohmygod." Kane is on one knee in front of me, holding his mother's ring, smiling.

"A marriage license. Will you marry me Wren?" Kane's eyes are full of love and promise *with a side of dirty sexy fun times sparkling in there.* I hold out a shaking hand and he slides the ring on my finger.

"Damn right, I will," my voice is full of tears, I didn't think it was possible to be this happy, "I'm giving you my heart."

"And I'm giving you mine, Baby," his voice is hoarse, holding back happy tears of his own, "keep it safe."

* * *

Next Up? Let's take a little trip to the beach.

〜

Finding My Sun
I'm Not Drunk, You're Drunk

Laurel

"Macie Moo, I lovvvve you," I hear my own voice over the pounding music and cringe, realizing the whiskey has taken over. Declaring how I feel for this man that is currently holding me up seems like the plan. Leaning back, it's clear that I would tip over if his arm wasn't around me, and I look into his eyes. *Instant regret.*

"You're smashed, Laurel," Mace's beautiful accent rolls over my skin. *It's honestly probably the thing about him that I do love.* His expression is wary. I don't know why I just told him I love him, actually. Seems like a thing to do. So does getting another drink, but he frowns and keeps ahold of me when I try to head for the bar.

Mace Carson, lean, inked, broody. He's a British rock star and he wants everyone to know it, *and I just called him Macie Moo and dropped an L-bomb. Shoot me now.* His eyes flicker over my shoulder, he waves a hand, and one of his security detail appear in my line of sight.

"She's making an idiot of herself, make sure she gets home," Mace extricates himself from my arms, "there's a good girl," he pats me on the ass and nods at his paid gorilla.

"Sure, Boss." The gorilla, I eventually recognize as Tim, gently takes my arm. I've taken two wobbly steps before my slushy brain can send a signal to my mouth.

"Wait, what the hell? Did I just get sent home? Are you fucking kidding me?" As I build up steam, Tim smoothly winds an arm around my waist. Literally picking me up, he carries me to the exit of the club. I'm too shocked to do much more than smack his head and shoulders with my phone. *How in hell have I not lost this thing yet?* Tim's an old pro though, he doesn't stop moving until we reach a sleek black car and he deposits me in the back seat.

"You'll thank me tomorrow, Miss Laurel," he grins and then politely ignores me while I pout in the back seat the entire drive. Pulling up to the entrance of my apartment building, Tim gets out and opens my door, offering me a hand and smoothly passing me on to the doorman. Job done, he gets back in the car and leaves.

"Hello, Ron." I gather the wilted shreds of my dignity about me and wish I'd had the foresight to take off, and carry, my heels. The car ride gave me a moment to sober up a tad and I feel like an ass.

"Evening, Miss Williams, do you need a hand upstairs?" He's trying to hide a smile and I'm grateful.

"No thank you, Ron, I'm fine," I prove it by walking steadily to the elevator and pushing the button. Stepping inside, I wait for the doors to close and rest my forehead on the cool metal panel above the buttons.

This isn't me.

Coffee As Art

❦

Laurel
  3 months later

Humming to myself, I juggle two coffees as I let myself into Mace's penthouse and kick off my shoes. Setting them on the counter, I blink as I see the lineup of empty bottles on the counter. *Somebody had a hell of a night.* It's not uncommon, just a little unusual for a Tuesday.

Ever since my embarrassing ride home, I've stepped back from the endless parties that swept me away when Mace and I started dating. Mace and I have realized that we connect on a deeper level. We've been exploring our relationship as he works on his next album. *I'm totally taking credit for that, I'm his muse.* We've slowed things down, *way...way down,* because Mace wants to concentrate on his music, and I've strictly avoided any repeats of the L-word.

The words are just flowing as Mace writes his new songs. It takes up all of his time, it's become his obsession. He's clearly inspired and his bandmates are anxious to get in the studio and start recording. *Probably the reason for all the bottles, they must have finally had a session last night.*

All of this time for thought and reflection has been good for me. *I keep telling myself that, otherwise I've just been doing a lot of yoga and trying not to die of boredom.*

I've started writing again too, resurrecting the blog that I began a few years ago while travelling with my father, I want to share it with Mace. I feel like it's time for him to start sharing in the things I'm interested in, branching out. I'd like him to travel with me, explore some new places. I'm nervous about bringing it up, but we care about each other, we need to keep growing together.

Leaving my bag on the counter, I pick up the coffees, crossing the living area as I head for the bedroom. Mace is probably still sleeping. As I walk down the hall, my feet sink into plush carpet, making no sound. Mace and I both startle as we meet at his bedroom door.

"Laurel, shit! Startled me Love!" Mace whispers, stepping into the hall and pulling the door shut behind him. *Weird.* He's got a shirt in his hand and he quickly pulls it over his head, running a hand through his hair.

"Hey, good morning," I tilt my head up and lean in to give him a kiss. He gives me the most perfunctory of pecks. *Weird.* He gingerly takes one of the coffees out of my hand.

"Cheers, Love, this is perfect, let's go sit by the pool," he takes my arm to steer me back out to the living room. *Weird, weird, weird.*

"You know what? I think you're acting weird, so I'd like to see what's behind door number one first." Pulling my elbow out of his grasp, I quickly turn the doorknob and push the door open. Mace steps in my line of sight, but not before I see a flash of black hair as someone disappears into the bathroom.

"Laurel, you don't-" Mace falters as I turn to him, but whatever my face is doing must be pretty fierce because he just gets out of my way. Stomping into the room, I raise my hand to knock on the bathroom door. It flies open before my knuckles make contact and I gasp.

"Gabs? What the? Why are you-?" I'm so confused to see her standing there, her brown eyes swimming with tears. *She's wearing Mace's robe. Why is she wearing Mace's robe?*

"I'm so sorry," she whispers, "I didn't want you to find out this way, we made a mistake..." Gabrielle flaps her hands helplessly as I stand there speechless. "Please, Laurel, can we-" she bites her lip, shaking her head as tears start to slide down her cheeks.

"Laurel, Love," Mace is trying for a soothing tone. "Let's go talk." Turning to look at him, I feel a smile stretching my lips. I back away from his outstretched hand, shaking my head slowly.

"Hmmm, that's a pass." Realizing I'm still holding my coffee, I take a sip. "Well shoot, it's gone cold." I whisper, and then before I can think too hard, I turn and throw it as hard as I can at the wall. It explodes, a beautiful splatter appearing on the white wool of the upholstered headboard, dripping down to soak the bedding. Gabs lets out a startled shriek. Mace is silent.

Nodding politely at each of them, I walk out of the room. I can feel their eyes on my back.

"Oh Laurel, I'm so sorry," I hear Gabrielle whisper my name sadly.

I've never been as damn proud of myself as I am right now. I don't scream at them and I will never let them see me cry. *Two-timing, faithless, wankers, they can have each other.* I simply put on my shoes, grab my bag and walk away from my new ex...and my new ex-best friend.

About the Author

Halo Roberts is a writer of steamy rom-coms, lover of coffee and dark beer, and spoiler of two fat cats affectionately known as the Bitchy Betas. She's living happily ever after in Iowa with her very own hunky farm boy, and a small herd of stubborn mules that look a lot like children.

Head on over to haloroberts.com, sign up for Halo's newsletter and receive a free download of her short story, A Night at the Diner.

You can connect with me on:

- http://haloroberts.com
- https://twitter.com/RobertsHalo
- https://www.facebook.com/halorobertsauthor
- https://www.bookbub.com/profile/halo-roberts
- https://www.instagram.com/halorobertswrites
- http://bit.ly/halogoodreads

Subscribe to my newsletter:

✉ http://haloroberts.com

Also by Halo Roberts

Sweet, steamy, laugh-out-loud romantic comedies that always end in a happily ever after...or two.

Finding My Night
Second star to the right...
A sassy chef with a crush on her boss finds herself on a 'not-a-date' with him in this hilariously steamy romp. Complete with a problematic socialite, a cream puff fiasco, and a killer dress with a strategic peek of lace, there might also be a man-bun...a pair of dueling best friends...and a wedding...or two.

Finding My One
Blue skies and dirt roads and peaches, oh my...

A real job with the family business or goodbye trust fund...my parents have lost their minds. The icing on this craptastic cake is setting up headquarters in some backwater southern town, complete with a partner...a rugged, country, single dad that flips every switch I've got...and a few I didn't know about. ~Veronica

Things are heating up in the country...

Finding My Safe
The songs say love is in the water... and strange...

When chance brings Wren and Kane together again, things have changed. Wren is graduating med school, soon to start her residency. Kane is a bouncer at a crappy roadside bar. When an ambush in an alley makes him depend on Wren far more than he expected, can they find love in the midst of five-dollar tequila shots, surprise proposals and the bright lights of Las Vegas?

Here's hoping love is also at Joe's bar...and not actually strange.

Finding My Sun
Breakups suck.

They suck even more after you drunkenly tell your A-list rock star boyfriend that you love him...then find your now ex best friend in his bed. Welcome to Laurel's world. So, what's a girl with a mangled heart to do? Escape to the Caribbean for some sun, sangria, and...a surfer?

Laurel meets Trey and sparks fly, hammocks flip, and all signs point to love. But when best friend and rock star drama invades the island, can new love last? Laurel has decisions to make, hearts to break and a sunburn to avoid in this two-part romantic comedy.